We can learn from insects if we are not too proud. Nature reinforces and expands our knowledge of God and His teachings.

The universe testifies of its Creator. The heavens declare His glory. The earth speaks of His providence. Both simple and complex living things bear witness to the One who is Lord of all life.

Of the ten plagues sent upon Egypt, three involved insects. But Pharaoh would not be instructed by the lice, the flies, the locusts.

And so he was punished. His land was devastated. His firstborn son died. His armies drowned in the waters of the Red Sea.

The author makes no apologies for the reminders he finds in the insect world that call attention to our spiritual needs and God's plan for our lives.

INSECT PARABLES

Robert J. Baker

HERALD PRESS
Scottdale, Pennsylvania
Kitchener, Ontario

INSECT PARABLES
Copyright©1976 by Herald Press, Scottdale, Pa. 15683
    Published simultaneously in Canada by Herald Press,
    Kitchener, Ont. N2G 4M5
International Standard Book Number: 0-8361-1337-3
Printed in the United States of America
Design: Alice B. Shetler

CONTENTS

AUTHOR'S PREFACE

From my boyhood experiences and my background as a science teacher I have tried to share in this book some of the spiritual lessons that I believe may be learned or reinforced by simple observations from the fascinating world of wings and exoskeletons.

Proverbs 6:6 says, "Go to the ant, O sluggard; consider her ways, and be wise." Perhaps Solomon, often considered the wisest of humans, wrote that simple proverb. In this book we would like to follow such advice. We can learn from insects, if we are not too proud.

God used insects to teach Pharaoh, but Pharaoh would not learn. Of the ten plagues sent upon Egypt, three of them involved insects. But Pharaoh would not be instructed by the lice, the flies, the locusts. And so he was punished, his land was devastated, his firstborn son died, his armies drowned in the waters of the Red Sea. God will teach us through varied media. He needs the opportunity, we need the openness.

I am personally convinced that nature reinforces and expands our knowledge of God and His teachings. I believe that the universe testifies of its Creator, that the heavens declare His glory, that this earth speaks of His providence, that both simple and complex living things bear witness to the One who is Lord of all life.

I know that we have the Holy Scriptures to tell us of God. I know that Jesus Christ came to reveal the Father to us, that the Holy Spirit glorifies that revelation. And yet I believe that in addition to such disclosures, we have much about us that is declaring either audibly or silently, singularly or in concert, that Jehovah is almighty, that Jesus is to be Lord, that the Holy Spirit seeks to operate in a fuller way in all of our lives. Not only is that world of nature declaring the Trinity, but it is also speaking to our relationships to both the Godhead and our fellowmen.

Can we see God in creation; can we hear creation speak to us? Paul in Romans 1:20 says that we are without excuse if we do not see God "in things that have been made." New truths are waiting to become visible before us. Strange as it seems, the invisible is apparent if we only open our eyes. I pray that God will use this book to make Himself and His will more clear and real to each reader.

Entomology, the study of insects, brings to our attention many six-legged examples that can become our instructors. The help God offers us, the lessons He would have us learn from insects, can be ignored. Jehovah offered Israel the use of His hornet armies to drive out the inhabitants of the Promised Land (Exodus 23:28-30), but the Israelites chose to murmur, to depend upon the arm of flesh, and it cost them dearly. I believe that God can help us through this book to again see His goodness and wisdom to us, to learn from His little creation about the Greatest Living One who ever was, or shall be—my Lord and yours.

Insects are the most numerous of all the animals in God's creation. Probably today they make up 80 percent of all the world's animals and they have not all been identified. Ross E. Hutchins, in his book *Insects*, states that more than 6,000 new species are discovered each year. Insects have adapted to life throughout the world and are found on every continent, including Antartica.

My interest in insects in recent years has led me to many books, and I have included a bibliography of some thirty of them. They are books that I have read, that I have skimmed, that have expanded my horizons and reinforced within me the consciousness that God's small creation has big lessons for us. Over the years ideas are dropped into one's mind through reading such books, through observation, through listening, through personal reflection. Those original ideas may be unrecognizable when they surface after long periods of submergence in one's mind, in this case, to let an insect speak to us. To footnote the original spark that lit the fire, that resulted in a chapter of this book, is impossible. My grateful thanks to each person, known or unknown, who has touched my life so that this book could be written.

In the Appendix I have listed the ten most common insect orders (orders are subgroupings under class groupings, which in turn are divisions under Phylum Arthropoda where insects are slotted in the animal world. Alas that science must be so technical!). Most of the insects discussed in this book will come from those ten common orders. I have also listed ten other orders, less common than the first ten. Several chapters in this book involve members of these minor orders. With each of the orders listed, whether they are major or minor, I have given several characteristics of that particular grouping and have named a few members of it. After 28 years of teaching science, it is difficult not to consider each reader as a pupil, each page of the book as an assignment. I have tried not to be too tedious in sharing that which has brought amazement and joy to me. I want the reader, along with me, to sense with awe how these tiny animals can speak to us about our Christian life. As a science teacher, however, I strive for accuracy, and accuracy at times demands an explanation beyond two-syllable words.

You may feel that the author in his insect investigations rather frequently finds his six-legged friends pointing to various aspects of the Christian witness, that the Holy Spirit is often woven into his moralizing. This is an accurate observation.

One should write out of his experience, out of his beliefs. As a Christian of four decades, I believe that there are two reliable bench marks against which to sight and thus effectively evaluate the progress of our Christian walk. The bench marks are: How successfully have we witnessed for that Galilean, how completely are we managed and moved by the Holy Spirit? Said a bit differently, a bit more personally: Has my life been a successful advertisement for Jesus Christ, have I come to terms with the Holy Spirit?

So, as you peruse these pages, I make no apologies for the variety of reminders I have found in the insect world that call my attention to our need to speak of Jesus, to accept from the Spirit whatever He has for us.

To me, that is what the Christian life is all about.

To think that a book is born through the efforts of a single person, someone grandly called the author, is sheer fantasy. Books come into being because of the cooperation, encouragement, and help of many.

My grateful thanks to several involved in this production:

Thank you, Lorene King, for typing the manuscript, parts of it several times because I never knew when to quit revising.

Thank you, Norval E. Adams, biology teacher of Elkhart High School, one who cared for me both when I was your pupil, then later as your teaching colleague. You are long gone, but somehow I believe you still are listening, smiling, caring.

Thank you, Dr. S. W. Witmer of Goshen College, for that course in entomology where dead grasshoppers came "alive."

Thank you, Wife Anna Mae and Daughter

Rebecca, because you forgave when I was so busy with my "bug book" that I neglected to be a husband and a father.

Thank you, God, for creating the living world, then handing to man a bit of Your creativity, enabling us to see in that tiny world of six-legged creatures, glimpses of both You and Yours. And, since You are mine, and I am Yours, that makes Your gift of double beauty. Thank You, Lord: You're the best.

Robert J. Baker
Elkhart, Indiana

1

Cases of
Mistaken
Identification

I am not certain where my boyhood friends and I got our names for insects. Perhaps it was from older boys who got them from older boys, who in turn had received them from older boys, and so on. For example, there was the "pill bug."

We called them pill bugs when we found them under rocks, under logs, occasionally just wandering feebly about under the dripping outside water faucet. They were gray in color, possessors of many feet, but slow movers. And when you picked them up, they rolled into a tight little ball that resembled a pill. To us they were another insect, one aptly named.

We identified the brown streaker that whizzed across the basement floor as the "thousand-legged worm." And we never picked them up, because they were "deadly poisonous." So we had been told. For that reason we were excused from counting their appendages to make sure that they had a thousand legs. Certainly they had a plenty; their locomotion was superb.

It is true that at that age, neither our insect classification nor our reaction to insects was very consistent. To us insects were anything small, something you swatted, stepped on, picked up, or fled from. Your actions sometimes depended upon what weapon was at hand and the limited and inaccurate knowledge you had of the fellow under observation. I suppose some of that reaction depended also upon how rapidly the adrenaline was flowing at that hour.

When we saw a spider at grandmother's house, it was to be quickly removed in a piece of cloth, preferably without damaging the spider. Cloth was used because Kleenex had not been invented and handkerchiefs were for girls. Grandma did not like spiders, but she had no intention of going against the proverb, "If you wish to thrive, let a spider run alive."

Perhaps the proverb was based upon the fact that spiders killed insects and were considered along with the ladybird beetle to be among the "good guys." The spider was considered by us to be a poor-looking good guy in the insect world.

Sometimes we caught a granddaddy longlegs. And in the process a leg might come off in our hand. Since he had eight, a loss of one seemed of little consequence. We would hold the amputated leg in our hand and watch its slight wiggles while the former owner ambled off, quite content with the seven remaining. We never knew that it was the least of his worries, that at his next molt ("skin changing") he would produce another leg.

To us he was just a funny member of the insect world that walked rather slowly, somewhat like grandpa.

Anyone who is familiar with the rudiments of insect identification knows that our pill bug, thousand-legged worm, spider, and granddaddy longlegs were not insects at all.

Insects have definite characteristics that rule out the four relatives above. Insects have three body segments, six legs, an external skeleton, often two pairs of wings, usually one pair of antennae.

None of the insect relatives we saw as boys qualified on all counts. The pill bugs (sow bugs would be more correct) belong to the class *Crustacea*. Their legs are too numerous, exceeding the insect's six by eight.

Our brown thousand-legged worms were really centipedes. We couldn't even keep our rough citizen nomenclature straight. Centipedes have only one pair of legs per body segment while millipedes have two pairs of legs on each body segment. The prefix "centi" refers to "hundred," the prefix "milli" suggests "thousand." Our brown scurrying friend was a centipede and the nickname "hundred-legged worm" would have been more correct. I suppose our boyish tendency to exaggerate caused us to pick the larger number as descriptive of the basement speedster.

Grandmother's spiders with eight legs and only two basic body segments definitely belong to *Class Arachnida* and not *Class Insecta*.

Our granddaddy longlegs is more correctly

called harvestman and his too numerous appendages immediately disqualifies him from ever belonging to the insects. Pulling off two legs doesn't do the job.

In the scientific world classification is a matter of grouping. We do not group by size, color, or habitat. Instead, we group by structural similarities.

Amateurs may have trouble in classifying correctly plants and animals, but a good taxonomist who specializes in such slotting of living things will doggedly proceed until he has the organism correctly categorized and nailed down.

How do we classify a Christian? If an animal has six legs, three body segments, an exoskeleton, and the like, then I've no question in my mind. I have identified an animal as an insect. True, some insects may have only one pair of wings, a few none, and at some life stages look very unqualified to be so named, yet as a whole it is not hard to slot an insect as an insect. Boyish mistakes could be excused. Now that I know the rules I do not err, for insects are "knowable." But a Christian? By what marks shall we identify him?

The Bible states that the early Christians were recognized by their love one for another. But there are non-Christians today who also possess the gift of indiscriminate love.

The scientific world is agreed on insect characteristics. Not so in the Christian world when it tries to say who is and who is not a Christian. We argue about the marks of such a breed.

Let me give you what I think to be the unquestionable marks of the Christian. I believe they lie deeper than a loving attitude, more accurate than even the gifts of the Spirit. The gifts of the Spirit can be simulated.

If a person has met Jesus Christ, recognized Him as God's official Mediator, found forgiveness through confession of sins, and is allowing Christ today to live through him, then he is a Christian. I don't care how many legs he has, whether he flies or not. The number of his body segments and complexity of skeletal system are the least of my worries. Such a person is my brother in Christ and I cannot confuse him with the *Barnacles* or *Spiders* of the world.

Insects are identifiable by their structural characteristics. For Christian identification I will need to go a bit deeper. The insect I can identify from the outside, but for the Christian I want to know what has happened within. The presence of Christ is the key for identifying the Christian. He who has Him will testify of Him. The presence of Christ cannot be hidden.

Someone has said, "If Christianity was a crime, and you were brought before a bar of justice because of being so accused, would there be enough evidence to convict you?" It's a sobering thought.

A professor's students decided to trick him. They took the body of one insect, glued to it wings, legs, and head from three separate other insects and asked him to identify it.

He looked at it carefully, saw their attempts to fool him, and acted puzzled. He asked, "When it was alive, did it hum?"

His students, feeling that the professor was being taken in by their forgery, said eagerly, "Yes, it did hum when in flight."

Then the one learned in insect lore and the ways of students said, "Why, gentlemen, then it is obvious: this is a humbug."

So it is with Christians. We may fool some of our fellowmen, perhaps all of them, but we cannot fool God. He will know us because we are His, not artificial creations by man, but creatures of the new birth. Praise God.

I am the door; if anyone enters by me, he will be saved, and will go in and out and find pasture. . . . I am the good shepherd; and know my own and my own know me. John 10:9, 14.

2

The
Upside-Down
Beetle

The beetles (the nonsinging variety, without long hair or guitars) are my favorites among the insects. *Order Coleoptera* is where they belong, varying in size and color, some good, some bad. Here is where the "ladybug" fits in, the orange-with-spots beetle which is really not a bug at all. And here is where the beautifully colored Japanese beetle can be found, pest that he is. But such a good-looking beetle with his bronze, green, and white markings!

The long-horned wood beetles trail their graceful antennae, the "gold bug" (*Catalpa lanigera*) glistens as he reminds me of Edgar Allan Poe's delightful short story, "The Gold Bug."

Perhaps my love for the beetles is responsible for my driving Volkswagens the last ten years. Or would an examining psychiatrist find other relationships? Such as the following: Many beetles are metallic in color, perhaps reminding me subconsciously of money and accelerating my love for them. I am not certain how many amateur entomologists are fond of beetles, certainly few farmers since my friends are notorious for their chewing, devouring mouthparts.

Among my beetle acquaintances are the click beetles. They vary from small brown or black fellows to the magnificent eyed elater which has two large spots on its inch-or-more-long body. The spots are on the insect's thorax, not the head, and have nothing to do with seeing. Those eye spots, however, may cause some birds to steer clear of this staring "menace."

Click beetles get their names from the sound they make. One may hear this "click" when he simply picks up the beetle, the noise causing the "picker-upper" to drop the clicker in surprise—which is exactly what he wants. But most often the click comes about when the beetle uses an interesting mechanism it has for righting itself. It is not so much an escape mechanism, but a technique for getting himself off his back and on his feet. While on his back, the beetle bends his thorax (chest part of the body) until it hooks a sharp spine into a notch on its abdomen. The action would compare to our lying on our back and doing sit-ups. Only in this case, when the beetle releases its self-cocking mechanism, it is hurled into the air because of the sudden re-release of the muscular tension. And more times than not it comes down right side up. Cats may land aright each time, but the click beetle is not so perfect. Mathematically, I suppose, on the basis of the beetle having one "top" and one "bottom," the odds of him coming down right side up should be one in two. Actually they beat those odds, more often than not, finding themselves more often than not on their six feet when they land.

When on his back, the click beetle doesn't give up. He puts forth some energy and gets straightened out. The click beetle has been known to play possum, but if the watcher is patient, he'll throw his mechanism into action and before your eyes you can see the little fellow go from flat on his back to an upright position in a flick of a click. If he has a somersaulting failure or two, he doesn't quit. He seems to know the odds, that after those failures the chances for success are bound to come, just around the next corner, just after the next "click."

A friend of mine is a Fuller Brush salesman. I talked to him about how frustrating it must be to go to a series of homes and in each case ring up a "No Sale."

He told me that it is not frustrating at all. He knows the odds. If he has a series of poor days, he knows that a series of good days will balance things out. He just keeps plugging away, puts even more energy into his sales' work, and ends up landing on his feet again.

Christians sometimes end up flat on their back, too. Our acceptance of Christ is no guarantee that we will not have problems. When they come, what should we do? We may lay there and wave our legs in despair like the giant sea turtle or we may spring back on our feet again like the click beetle.

Norman Vincent Peale is sometimes criticized for not being a realist. I believe Mr. Peale is a realist, a realist who recognizes that God is for *real*. And with such a philosophy, such an outlook, one can believe in the power of positive thinking.

When we are down, our God is available for us to call upon. We never get a busy signal when we ring His number. When we are flat on our backs, physical or spiritual, when the world seems upside down, He knows. Actually it is not the world that is upside down, but only ourselves. The One who created this world still has it under His control. He still rules. From Him comes the power to raise us up, to place us on our feet, to see the world from a new perspective.

The click beetle must lift his head and thorax up in order to engage the spring in the notch in its abdomen. It is only then that muscular energy can be harnessed and later released which will flip the click beetle over. When we bend our wills as well as our knees before Him, when we lift our heads to Him, God provides the energy to set us aright.

From the lowly click beetle, I learn what to do when I am "down." I reach out to God, draw up-righting power from Jesus Christ, Lord of my life.

He drew me up from the desolate pit, out of the miry bog, and set my feet upon a rock, making my steps secure. Psalm 40:2.

3

The
Costly
Mistake

Some years ago a friend drove his freshly polished car to my home in an attempt to get an explanation for a mysterious development on a door panel of that car.

He showed me what was puzzling him and it was intriguing to say the least. Running in a fairly straight line diagonally across that door were forty to fifty tiny pinhead size spheres cemented on quarter inch filaments projecting out from the polished surface. What were we seeing?

The golden-eyed lacewing insect is well named, having pale green gossamer-like wings that contrast nicely with its yellow eyes. Although the lacewing insects look delicate, their appetite is not. Their ravenous healthy appetite keeps them feeding on aphids and other small insects, the larvae so greedy they are called "aphis lions."

The most distinctive trait of this insect, however, is the way the female lays her eggs. She usually deposits them on leaves so that when the young larvae hatch from the eggs they will have plenty of food at hand. But the eggs are not deposited directly upon the leaf. Instead, the female secretes from her abdomen a tiny drop of gelatinous liquid which she then draws out by raising her posterior end. The thread quickly hardens and upon the upper end of the stalk she now cements an egg. She usually does this for all her eggs; thus when the operation is complete we see those eggs standing like tiny lights upon their individual lampposts.

Why does the golden-eyed lacewing choose this strange, unorthodox method of egg placement? Some entomologists believe it is because of the fact that when the young lacewing larvae hatch from their eggs, they are quite willing to feast upon their unhatched brothers and sisters. If they were not safely perched on their tiny "tree houses" they might eat each other up!

So now we know what the tiny pinhead objects were on the thread size stalks that my friend found on his car. But why were they there? Why did the golden-eyed lacewing place her eggs on the side of a car? When the young would hatch in five to twelve days, no tiny aphids were likely to be found on the painted surface for them to feed upon. Had mother lacewing made a mistake?

Yes, she had—an understandable mistake, but a fatal one for her children. Remember, the car had been freshly polished. Sitting in the sun, the door panel must have reflected, mirrorlike, the leaves from a nearby tree. And this particular egg-laying insect mistook the reflection for the real thing. It was a mistake that provided an interesting object lesson to my friend and me.

How often we are fooled as Christians. We see things around us that are not real, permanent, nor lasting. They are reflections only from carefully polished surfaces. We sample them, try them, and imagine that they are genuine, but they are only artificial—attractive but deceptive limitations which beguile us. The tragedy is that our children often are the ones to suffer.

Satan uses many tricks to beguile us. He is a master at deception, presenting to us tempting reflections, suggesting to us that we hew out new cisterns. But they turn out to be broken cisterns that can hold no water. And our children thirst.

The golden-eyed lacewing was fooled. She yielded to a reflection, and her egg laying efforts were wasted. Perhaps as a parent of today the polished surface that attracts me is materialism. When I substitute such a fleeting, dancing, temporal thing of this world for the reality of God's grace and mercy, I'm a loser. But worse yet, my children are losers.

Our insect friend who chose a reflection in place of the genuine could be excused. Her elementary nervous system permitted no thinking. As Christian parents, our responsibility is of a higher level. When we place our children in a sterile, hostile environment where they will suffer spiritual hunger, perhaps even starvation, God will hold us accountable.

Perhaps every polished and shiny car should be a reminder to me as a parent that I can give my children all the things of this world, but nothing can compare with the satisfaction and happiness that will come to them through a personal relationship with Jesus Christ. He is genuine, not a reflection.

For my people have committed two evils: they have forsaken me, the fountain of living waters, and hewed out cisterns for themselves, broken cisterns, that can hold no water. Jeremiah 2:13.

The
Pious
Tiger

All insects are characterized by having six legs, but not necessarily for locomotion. The praying mantis, for example, uses only the last two pairs for supporting and moving his long, slender body. As he moves, the first pair do not come in contact with the ground. Instead, they are held elevated, bent, and raised as if in supplication, begging, seeking. And because their position resembles a person in an attitude of prayer, the praying mantis has been so piously named.

He is one of our larger insects, often measuring three to four inches in length. And if he were not so well camouflaged by greens and browns, if he did not have the habit of remaining almost motionless for long periods of time, more of us would have seen this fascinating member of *Order Orthoptera*, where he is thrown rather unceremoniously in with his poorer relatives, the grasshoppers and cockroaches. But, surely most of us have seen pictures of the insect, those front legs raised as if he was in the process of saying grace at the banquet table or rendering the benediction at church.

This arthropod is special in several ways. He is the only insect that can move his head like a human. And that characteristic in itself makes him an entertaining fellow to watch. His triangular head is set with the usual two large compound eyes. And as he sits quietly, either waiting for a meal or munching methodically on one at hand, that triangular appendage swivels about, checking his surroundings with care. One almost expects to see him nod to you as you observe, to say a few words of greeting in insect language. But he makes no sound. Some insects "speak" through vibrating wings or membranes. But the praying mantis sits like a specter, ghostlike. He is quiet, but, oh so observant.

Although he is perfectly harmless to humans, he is a terror in the insect jungle, the silent predator that enjoys not only lunching on other insects, but is willing to take on small frogs, snakes, salamanders, or even to battle a sparrow. Size means nothing to him.

Despite our wandering interest in this creature, our attention often returns to those uplifted forelegs that instinctively remind us of a monk or priest at prayer. Casual observers, for instance, would not dream that this gentle appearing insect will calmly bite through neck nerve ganglia of his captured victim, and then proceed to devour his immobilized meal, section by section, live tissue by live tissue. And as he eats, he turns

that versatile attached head about to any specta-
tors as if to say, "Very tasty. You can't beat having fresh grasshopper for breakfast."

The female praying mantis is not at all adverse
to devouring her husband after mating. And
when several male suitors are about, often one or
so of them follow her husband through that
simple digestive tract.

Certainly, appearances are deceiving. Those
front legs are especially adapted not only for seiz-
ing, but also for retaining her captured meal.
Strong spines line the two sections of the leg that
clamp together and few insects can escape before
she neatly anesthetizes them with that "spinal"
severance. It has been suggested that the praying
mantis should be renamed the "preying mantis."
It would be more accurate, more truthful.

If biblical peoples would be given insect roles,
surely the Pharisees of the New Testament would
play the part of the praying mantis. Their appearance was deceptive; they were real "foolers."
But they did not fool Jesus. Both Jesus and John
the Baptist had some hard words for those pious
hypocrites of that day. They went around with
enlarged borders on their garments, with
broadened phylacteries according to Matthew,
arms raised in public prayers. But they sought to
be seen of men, not of God. They devoured
widow's houses, and barred men from the
kingdom of God. Their long prayers were only a
pretense. Their outward appearance of piety did
not mislead Jesus. He called them whitewashed
sepulchers, camouflaged containers of dead
men's bones.

I suppose that hypocrites, like the poor, are always with us. Undoubtedly, there are such people in every congregation through the religious world. Their demeanor, their attitude, give false impressions. Their saintly pretense, like the posture of the praying mantis, is not for real.

As Christians, our primary task is not to judge our fellow believers. Our primary task is to live for the One for whom we were named, Jesus Christ. But we owe it to ourselves, to the church, to the world, to submit ourselves one to another in the fellowship of believers for counsel and advice. Sometimes others can help us to see where we are artificial, veneered over. When the Holy Spirit reveals to us where we are not genuine, then we need to excise from our lives any actions and attitudes that are only fillers and frills, carried out to impress others or ourselves. Being a Christian is too serious a business to be in it on a part-time basis.

If one studies the praying mantis a bit, watching him at his deadly work, one quickly sees that appearances can be deceiving. He looks like a bishop saying his prayers, when actually he is muttering to himself, "Whom can I eat next?"

It is easy on Sunday to look very much the Christian, very "disciplish." But how are we during the week, from Monday to Saturday, living in our homes, working at our jobs, dealing with the nitty-gritty of life? The sinner is more likely to see us in our weekday roles than he is on Sunday in church. Is the picture the same? The question is serious.

Undoubtedly some sinners justify their position

because they have been turned off by hypocrites in the church. They have seen the false fronts erected by such synthetic Christians, recognized that they are like cheap chocolate Easter bunnies, hollow inside. Unfortunately, such observers often judge the entire Christian church by a few members who are noticed to be only empty shells, gingerbread Christians with lots of trimmings, beautiful facaded, with little behind them. Like an insect fooled by the pious-looking praying mantis, some outside the church have been seriously hurt by Christians who are only acting out their Christianity.

Without doubt the church is not perfect. Someone with tongue in cheek has compared the church with Noah's ark: "If it weren't for the storm outside, you couldn't stand the stink inside." This may be a bit exaggerated, but there is enough truth to it that a Christian cannot laugh too loud.

The praying mantis is a wolf in sheep's clothing. As Christians we are called to a life of integrity, transparency. To be less than that is to be dishonest; it is to be classified as a hypocrite.

If we want to be honest with ourselves and with one another, I believe that the Holy Spirit will point out to a Christian when he is not "practicing what he is preaching." And when He does, then we must change. There will be no hypocrites in heaven.

What is the hope of the godless ... when God takes away his life? Job 27:8.

5

An
Early
Astronaut

They called it the black death, and it swept Europe in the 1300s, resulting in the loss of one quarter of that continent's population. The disease is a form of the bubonic plague. In 1907 it was proven that fleas carried on rats were responsible for transferring the disease to man. The moving of rats from port to port by ships enables the disease to jump large bodies of water and infest new areas miles from the original epidemic. A greater care in seaports to keep rats from either entering or leaving a ship has largely reduced the hazard of the disease, serving to keep it isolated where it can be more easily controlled.

Many of us who have pets have likely had some acquaintanceship with fleas. Our cat, named Twilight because she was gray in color, introduced them to our basement. As long as she carried adult fleas in her own fur, it was her problem, and I do not recall any of us being acutely conscious of her troubles. But soon the adult fleas laid eggs and the flea population on the basement floor far exceeded the number for which Twilight could adequately care. They lay in wait on that basement floor for anyone who crossed their domain. Since adult fleas need blood, they leaped at the chance for ours.

The leap for so small a fellow is tremendous. They can project themselves a full thirteen inches. A human being who can high jump six feet, or his own height, is doing quite well. Since the flea is only .04 of an inch tall, this means that he is leaping over 300 times his own height. If a human could duplicate this ability it would mean we could at one leap scale an 1,800-foot barrier, a leap of about a quarter of a mile. Superman of the comics would be for real.

By spraying our basement floor and dusting Twilight we soon eliminated the flea problem from both ourselves and the cat. But the memory still remains of how I sampled the basement with legs bared to the knees to check for the presence of our enemies. And as I walked about, as if by magic the tiny black dots appeared on my feet, ankles, and even the calves of my legs. What power of leaping those fleas possessed!

We measure the thrust of rocket-powered spacecraft in terms of G's (earth gravities). An astronaut typically can expect to be subjected to perhaps seven G's. This means that the force exerted upon his body is equivalent to seven times that of the earth's pull of gravity. But it is estimated that the flea's blast off from our basement floor to my leg may reach an acceleration of 140 G's! And he does it without a space suit or chair molded to the contours of his tiny flea body.

Insects are designed for their environment. The flea's body is very hard and very thin from side to side with a vertical thinness just the opposite of the bedbug's horizontal flatness. And for the flea that works nicely. His skinniness means that he can slither through the dog or cat fur with ease.

That slender body is extremely tough. If he lights on your arm or leg, your best bet is to moisten a finger and trap him in the stickiness of your own saliva—and then proceed to grind him ruthlessly to flea powder. It will take more than a light indentation with the finger nail to finish him off. He's tough.

Fleas are not only strong—they are trainable. We have heard of flea circuses where the flea performs by pulling tiny wagons and chariots.

Fleas have no close relatives in the insect world, and for that reason are placed by themselves in *Order Siphonaptera*. Since the first part of that formidable word spells "siphon," we can easily remember where the flea belongs by thinking of his blood drinking habits. He siphons from us the "gas" that provides the energy to make those prodigious jumps of his that project him with such skill to his warm-blooded host.

The flea's magnificent leap for food is based on his ability to "cock" his third pair of legs under his body and trigger their release in a flea's breath of time. The unsnapping of those legs is like the release of a spring and the astronaut flea

leaves his basement "earth" and makes a successful landing on a "moon" ankle.

Yes, the flea leaps for his food. If he doesn't
land on the likes of me or my cat, he starves. The
Christian too needs to leap into God's Word for
feeding. If he doesn't, he starves; he spiritually
dies.

The Bible is full of admonitions for us to make
this leap. We are to study to make ourselves ap-
proved to God. We are to hide God's Word in
our hearts that we might not sin against Him. We
are to carry that Word as a sword, to use it as a
lamp, a light to our path. We are admonished to
go in the path of His commandments, to walk in
the law of the Lord, to take heed according to the
Word, to meditate in His precepts, to delight in
His statutes.

We are to search the Scriptures, to give ear and
hearken to the Word of the Lord. We are to keep,
retain, observe, and comfort one another with
the Word of God.

If we are not thirsting often after this water of
life, if we are not hungering continually after this
bread of life, our spiritual health may be failing.
A flea that is not leaping after his meal is either
full or sick. A Christian who is not leaping into
God's Word is likely either full or sick too. If he's
full, saturated with that Word, fine. But even as
we find it necessary to partake of the physical
food at regular intervals, so the Christian must
periodically be feeding upon the Bible. One meal,
even if it is a feast, doesn't provide nourishment
for long.

I never heard of a flea that took a half-hearted

jump. I doubt if there is such an "animal." I believe that the fleas who found me in our basement put their whole heart and soul into that leap. They did not with reluctance cock those rear legs and dispiritedly trigger off the "explosion" that wheeled them into their space adventure. Those fleas that found me were alert, purposeful, energetic, enthusiastic.

We can take some lessons from the flea. When he leaps for his meal, he puts forth a gigantic effort. If he would fill his stomach with my blood, nothing must interfere. He can't be so engrossed in checking out dust particles on the floor that he misses the opportunity at hand.

Each Christian needs to put forth every effort to make that soul-filling leap that lands him smack-dab in the middle of God's Word. My feeling is that it is a daily necessity to make such a feeding. We should be willing to leap over any obstacle, through any distance, to find the spiritual food we need for our survival as Christians.

> The law of the Lord is perfect, reviving the soul; the testimony of the Lord is sure, making wise the simple; the precepts of the Lord are right, rejoicing the heart; the commandment of the Lord is pure, enlightening the eyes; the fear of the Lord is clean, enduring forever; the ordinances of the Lord are true, and righteous altogether.
>
> More to be desired are they than gold, even much fine gold; sweeter also than honey and drippings of the honeycomb.
>
> Moreover by them is thy servant warned; in keeping them there is great reward. Psalm 19:7-11.

Prowling Parasites of the Night

The bedbug is in general a forbidden subject to discuss. Most of us claim total ignorance of this fellow. To show any familiarity with him might indicate that one has had firsthand experience with this blackguard of the insect world. It is true that through the use of modern insecticides today we have fewer "buggy" homes, but our quietness goes beyond that. Bedbugs are associated with unclean homes, hotels, and other sleeping establishments. So we plead ignorance of the subject. To have had bedbugs in one's home is considered a disgrace.

During the depression years of the early 1930s our family was several times disgraced. Those were difficult years and my widowed mother was trying to keep the family together, renting a home wherever possible, staying until we were evicted for failing to pay the rent, then moving on, the cycle often repeating itself.

In these rented homes, we often found that not all the former occupants had moved out. Our warm bodies in the beds quickly coaxed the bedbugs from the cracks in the floor, from behind the woodwork and loose wallpaper. When the lights were out, the silent army would attack. Authorities say that bedbugs often seek out their victims just before dawn, but our bedbugs seem to follow a more free schedule. They visited us any hour of the night. We became the host, they were the parasites. Although bedbugs are reported to respond to heat and smell, most authorities feel that such sensations are effective only within a few inches of the bug. Most of their victims are found simply through the bedbug's wanderings. As one of those victims, I thought they wandered my way rather frequently.

The adult bedbug is a flat, oval insect about 6 millimeters long. They are reddish brown in color and in warm temperatures are prolific breeders. Maturity comes in four to six weeks depending upon the temperature. Three or four generations may arise per year. When it "bites." the bedbug injects a fluid that prevents coagulation of the blood from the host. Actually the bedbug "pierces" instead of "bites." Tiny stylets (piercing mouth parts) penetrate with ease through the skin to the blood meal awaiting. The only evidence of the intrusion is a possible welt that may be noticed the next morning at the point of the bloodletting.

I remember as a boy how mother set each bed leg in a tin can with a bit of kerosene in the bottom of it. It was a moat through which the bedbug supposedly would not move. But they managed to circumvent it by one method or another and found us.

My brothers and I had a cruel revenge. Objecting to being used for giving bedbug transfusions, we sought our captors at night with pins, finding them on the sheets, in the mattress folds where they sought hiding. We speared their tiny flat bodies (round if they already had their evening meal) and callously finished them off on the flame from the kerosene lamp. We had no sympathy for our tormentors.

Probably by mother's persistent spraying and an occasional fumigation, more than by our periodic spearing, the bedbugs were conquered in each house and we would enjoy peaceful sleeping until our next adventure in moving into an empty house that held the dormant parasites. Bedbugs can easily go for months without feeding and so when we arrived, we were the feast that broke the famine.

Bedbugs may be scarcer today than they were when I was a boy, but they are still around. At one time they were not found in this country. They were unknown to the American Indian. Probably they arrived from England by ship. It is thought that originally they came from the Mediterranean Sea area of Southern Europe. Julius Caesar's legions are rumored to have brought them to England from the continent.

We have used the word "parasite" and the word "host" in talking about the bedbug. "Parasite" as applied to a person is not considered to be a very flattering description.

When used in description of a person it refers to "one who lives at another's expense." In the general biological world it is a "plant or animal living in, on, or with some other plant or animal at whose expense it obtains food and shelter."

The bedbug certainly deserves to be cataloged as a parasite. He found shelter in our homes, food from our bodies.

The animal or plant that provides the shelter or food, or both, is known as the "host." And "host" has a good connotation. When we host guests in our home, we consider our act to be one of graciousness, of hospitality. Hosts are the "good guys," parasites are the "bad guys." It is interesting to apply these two terms to the Christian church. Can a church have "parasites" within it? If so, what identifies them? And in such a case, who becomes the "host"?

Second Thessalonians 3:10 would lead us to believe that there were parasites in the church at Thessalonica. And the Apostle Paul was quite hard on them. He suggested that if they made no contribution, they should not eat. I cannot believe that Paul was speaking of the aged, the infirm, those unable to work. Evidently there were people in the church that were taking advantage of the early church's "having all things in common." Every new movement picks up those who want to ride free.

It has been my experience as an active elder in the church to find that in the typical assembly of believers there will be people with needs. And I refer now more to the physical need aspect. We are admonished to care for the widows and orphans, to give the cup of cold water without expecting a return. We are to care especially for those in the household of faith. And we have a responsibility that reaches outside the church. Surely none of us would quarrel with this. But the church must never make people dependent upon itself. We foster dependence upon Jesus Christ, not the church. By going back to the biological world we may learn something further in this regard.

In the biological world parasites have to be parasites or they can't make it. For example, in case of the tapeworm, it has no digestive system. It simply absorbs food from its host. It has no circulatory system, only a primitive reproductive system. Some scientists theorize (and this is important as we transfer some of our "parasite thinking" over to the church) that parasites represent degenerated life. They assume that body parts once possessed by ancestors of present-day parasites have been lost through lack of use. Perhaps the bedbug was once a responsible, respectable bug, making his own way in the world of insects. He may have chomped away on plants like other decent insects. Then he found man and other animals to be a soft touch. And so generation after generation he supped on them until his own body degenerated into nothing much more than a container for holding blood.

Would this suggest that Christians in the church who are continually and totally dependent on fellow members for a long period of time might become immune to work? Would it indicate that when the church only hands out help to people in the community, a short-range need may be met, but if the process continues we encourage a dependency upon the church which is not healthy? Is it sometimes easier to give $10 to a needy person in place of sitting down with him for planning and counsel?

By such questioning we open ourselves up to the accusation that we are middle-class bigots, people who have succeeded in life and expect others to do likewise, that we are anti-welfare, anti-Aid-to-Dependent Children. Such accusations can help us analyze our feelings. The question that faces the church on such issues is not whether it should minister to those with needs, but how it can best offer that cup of water in the name of Christ. As suggested, the cash donation is often the easy way out. At times it is the only way out and must be given by the church with that same gracious spirit which permeated all the living acts of the One we follow. But to give without thinking is not true Christian giving. It is too much like paying taxes, often a cold and painful action. It can be a technique for easing our own conscience rather than meeting the need of another.

Does the church today in the name of charity create parasites? To be as wise as serpents, as harmless as doves in this area is a formidable task. If we fail to open our hearts of compassion to one who has need, 1 John 3:17 suggests that we are lacking in the very love of God. Yet, if we minister only to man's immediate physical needs, creating in him a welfare syndrome, failing to touch his soul, then we may cause within him a vacuum into which seven devils could rush, and his second state might well be worse than the first.

The church should not be encouraging parasitism, producing "bedbug Christians." If the bedbug actually did degenerate, those early hosts did them no favor. Today the bedbug is so dependent upon warm-blooded mammals that he cannot stand upon his own six legs. We must not dehumanize our fellowmen by making them receivers only. Every person deserves the thrill of being productive. "Help ups" should replace "hand outs."

The church is to help people stand up, not lie down.

In all things I have shown you that by so toiling one must help the weak, remembering the words of the Lord Jesus, how he said, "It is more blessed to give than to receive." Acts 20:35.

Let the thief no longer steal, but rather let him labor, doing honest work with his hands, so that he may be able to give to those in need. Ephesians

7

The
Maker of
Ping-Pong Balls

Under the oak trees we sometimes find papery balls, perhaps an inch to an inch and a half in diameter. Upon occasion some of my pupils in junior high school bring these strange findings into the classroom, wondering what they could possibly be. They are quite light in weight, not white like our table tennis balls, but tan in color. They are approximately the same size, nearly spherical, but not possessing the elasticity of the ball with which the Chinese are so proficient.

Sometimes as the students and I examine them, we find a tiny hole on the surface. Either something has crawled in or something has crawled out of our puzzler.

Whether there is an external hole or not, we usually operate. To dissect our biological Ping-Pong ball is relatively simple. The papery covering is easily pierced and we find that it is supported by a fuzzy-like structure which seems to radiate out from a small, firm body at the center. The center object is about the size of a soup bean and extremely hard. Our nucleus may or may not have a discernible hole in it. Now the pupil or teacher surgeon must put on the pressure to make the penetration.

When our "soup bean" is opened, we find a small cavity at the center. And once when we performed this additional operation, a small insect glared up at us as if to rebuke us for our intrusion, then testily flew away. Very interesting to us, very fortunate for him that our scalpel did not dissect him. It was bad enough that we wrecked his home. But how did he ever get inside that hard center portion, which lay inside the fuzzy filling, which lay inside the papery covering?

What our students have found are "oak apples" more correctly known as oak galls. These productions again are one of the fascinating happenings that occur in the world of insects.

Plant galls in general are sometimes called "plant cancer." In the case which we have described above, a small wasp deliberately lays an egg between the upper and lower epidermis of the leaf. This in itself is quite an engineering feat but the wasp, *Amphibolips confluentes*, apparently has few failures.

Some plant gall students feel that the mother wasp injects also a bit of irritant from her body that promotes the growth of the gall. Others feel that the irritant comes from the young insect larva after the egg hatches. Since some of the gall producing wasps can cause a "Ping-Pong ball" to form by just stinging the leaf, the former theory seems to be the most acceptable.

The plant responds to the irritant by walling off the infected area. So the oak galls my students bring in represent basically plant tissue. The hole we find in some of our "Ping-Pong balls" marks the spot where the full-grown insect has emerged. And the tiny fly-like creature we found inside one of our center pieces was the adult wasp that we delivered by Caesarean section.

Unfortunately, some Christians are too much like the gall insects. We are responsible for the creation of walls. And we do it because we are irritating.

In Christianity there are many delicate razor edges, spiritual tight-ropes to walk. My Christian witness is one of those razor edges I need to walk with care. I should be bold in my testimony of Jesus Christ, but I should not be without tact. I should be a spokesman when the Spirit prompts, but I should not run ahead of God. I should be present with help when the person with whom I work has need, but I should not make a nuisance of myself. I should be insistant without being overbearing.

I walk the tightrope not only with the personality with whom I am directly dealing, but also the bystanders involved. Winning souls is seldom done in a closet. If I help lead one into the light of the gospel, but in the process turn off three others, have I gained or lost in the long run? The gall insect cares not that she ruins an oak leaf in the process of gaining one offspring. She cares not about barriers erected, about fallen oak galls, about "stung" leaves where not even an egg is laid and reproductive efforts are 100 percent nil. As a Christian, I care.

Jesus knew when to speak strongly to the Pharisees, the hypocrites of His day. He knew when He had reached the point of no return in His dealings with them, when to relax, when to put on the pressure, when to plead, when to demand. I am not so wise. As I witness, I need to pray for the wisdom of Solomon.

Sometimes through reviewing past experiences when we saw those walls go up, we may find the common denominator present that acted as the irritant.

Sometimes a group of fellow Christians can sit down with us and gently determine where we are "turning people off," where we are winning the battle but losing the war.

A gall insect works by instinct; she cannot change. I can. I may be living my Christian life without consciousness of poor habits, of being in a rut, of repeatedly offending others. I may need help from outside myself, people mirrors that reflect back what I am projecting. And that may hurt, to see oneself so pictured. To be earnest, to try and be a soul winner, then to learn that you irritate more than you anoint can be a real kick in the teeth. But it can be an instructive kick.

Irritating Christians are not good advertisements for the kingdom. They are not bearing the fruit of the Spirit. We are commanded to live peacefully with all men, if it is at all possible. Such living may depend upon the amount of His grace that rests within us. If there is not enough grace, enough wisdom, then I need to ,pray for a replenishing from above.

The plan of salvation has no allowances within it for "lump making" by Christians. We are to be "healers," not "hurters." We must be involved in the act of promoting spiritual reproduction without allowing any irritants from us to "cancerize" innocent bystanders.

If as Christians we are rubbing people the wrong way, it may be that the Lord needs to sandpaper us down to the place where our rough spots are gone. It may be painful, but it may be the very thing for which we need to pray.

Behold, I send you out as sheep in the midst of wolves; so be wise as serpents and innocent as doves. Matthew 10:16

8

The Insect with Intestinal Inhabitants

We have all heard the strange stories about how the housewife sits down at the table to relax, places her elbows upon it, and it collapses. Or the man who steps into the house and drops unceremoniously into the basement without benefit of elevator services. Or the librarian who opens the book and finds that the pages have disappeared from between the covers.

A number of stories such as these are true. Termites love wood and wood products, but abhor light and drying air. So they work from within, chewing away contentedly the interior of table legs, eventually only a thin layer of wood and varnish remain. The rest has been honeycombed out by munching termites. So when the weary housewife sits down to take her morning coffee break, the table collapses like a house of cards.

Termite damage runs into the millions of

dollars per year in the United States. Any termite scare in the neighborhood brings the pest exterminating trucks roaring to the premises with promises to save your house from providing free lunch for a host of hungry termites.

Unfortunately, swarming ants occasionally spread a false alarm. The ant is thin waisted, his abdomen pinched down to almost a thread where it joins the rest of the body. Termites are thick bodied throughout. The two pairs of wings of the termite are of equal length and size while those of the ant when they are in that flying stage are not.

Termites are seldom seen, but the mud tunnels which they build along a cement foundation to bridge the gap from the earth to the wood above are a dead giveaway for indicating the presence of the intruders. Since, as we mentioned, the termite avoids the light except at swarming time, the mud tunnel provides a dark passageway, safe from the drying air, through which he may journey to his wooden feast of floor joists, wall studding, dining room table, and other cellulose delicacies in the house above. Termites are not choosy about the kind of wood they consume and have been known to eat away a walnut gunstock or the ash of a baseball bat with equal relish.

One needs to be careful before saying that termites have no redeeming graces. Since most species are found in the tropics, they do hasten the decay cycle for fallen trees and other dead vegetation, acting as gardeners in clearing the forest floor. The large varieties are considered very tasty food in some parts of Africa. They are roasted over a slow fire and are regarded as being both finely flavored and nourishing. I am sorry that I cannot vouch for this. The America termites are much smaller and do not build the elaborate "hill" homes they do in the tropics which make them more easily found. So I have been relieved of sampling the roasted termite to verify that they belong on the restaurant menu.

Termites are thought to have an extremely good nose for wood. Certainly not an eye for it. The termites have a caste system and the soldiers and workers who make up the majority of the colony members are both wingless and sightless.

The more interesting question involved with the termite to me seems to be, "How can one subsist on a diet of wood?" Wood basically is composed of cellulose and lignin, plus some minerals, sugar, and resin. The cellulose which makes up sixty percent of the wood is considered indigestible to nearly all animals, large or small, and termites are no exception. Then how does the termite make it, rearing large families, comfortably hollowing out our homes as he exists on a diet of wood?

If the termite cannot digest wood, how can he live on it? The secret is found in the intestine of the termite. Living within those slender termite intestines are tiny one-celled inhabitants known as protozoa. These minute one cellers are responsible for digesting the cellulose for the termite. Members of the termite caste system that have no such protozoa in their body (such as kings, queens, and certain wingless "nobility") are fed predigested cellulose secreted by fellow termites who have the helpful protozoa in their bodies.

It's a neat partnership. The termites provide the protozoans with a comfortable home with an inside view, plus plenty of raw materials upon which to "chew." And the protozoans pay their rent faithfully by converting the cellulose into a digestible form of food that the termite can use.

The relationship between the termite and the protozoa is a good example of what is known in biology as symbiosis. Symbiosis is a partnership between two organisms who join together for mutual benefit. The dictionary says that symbiosis is "the living together in intimate association of two dissimilar animals, two dissimilar plants, or an animal and plant, ordinarily in an association advantageous, or often necessary to one or both, as the relation of an alga and a fungus forming a lichen."

In the case of the lichen, a plant, we have an alga and a fungus, two extremely different plants, living together quite contentedly. They have separate housekeeping chores, a real sharing of duties . The fungus provides the moisture, the house, so to speak, while the alga produces food for both of them. Everyone is happy.

The termite and protozoa could not ask for a nicer arrangement. Transfer of essential protozoa can be made from a termite "with them" to one "without them." Any termite without them is doomed to starvation or to be continually fed by fellow members of the colony.

In our brief look at the bedbugs, we found that

they were parasites. And we hoped not descriptive of the typical church member. But symbiosis is a different ball game, a beautiful illustration of the church. In the body of the believers we should have members living together in a mutual sharing situation.

How far should this sharing go? For some, such as the Hutterites, it is a system that reaches out into almost all areas of their living together. They practice a common ownership of goods, attempting to follow Acts 2:44. It becomes a king-size experiment in symbiosis among people. For them it seems to be working.

Most of us in the church world carry on our symbiotic relationships on a more limited scale. But surely they will be carried on. The fellowship of Christian believers is a caring one in which there should be many interrelationships that result from genuine concern.

And in those interrelationships each group benefits from such symbiotic relationships. We share the work load in the church, doing things for one another. We are not parasites upon one another, but rather partners one to the other.

Surely we see this manifested in the church in times of illness, death, financial loss, family crisis, and the like. At such times the ties among us grow ever stronger.

Perhaps the conventional, average body of believers should be thinking of new ways to become involved with fellow Christians in ordinary times instead of waiting for the time of crisis.

Perhaps for some of us it should become more of a way of life. Perhaps house churches are teaching us something in this regard. Certainly symbiosis is a better description of the church than parasitism. The body of Christ should be sharing and bearing, not striving and depriving.

And all who believed were together and had all things in common; and they sold their possessions and goods and distributed them to all, as any had need. Acts 2:44, 45.

9

Death
By
Design

Breathes there a boy with soul so dead,
Who never to his mother said,
  "Can I go barefoot?"

> —Apologies to Sir Walter Scott in
> "Lay of the Last Minstrel!"

Each year has many memorable events in it,
some fixed like our holidays, some determined
by events which pop into our lives unscheduled,
and some events that are dependent upon the
weather. Among those latter days was the first
warm day of spring when we dared with hope to
ask our mother if we might go barefoot for the
first time that year.

And if she said, "Yes," it was a real treat to
kick off the shoes with which we had been bur-
dened for the past six months and once more feel
the good earth between our toes.

Around our home the grass grew thin and dandelions abounded. About the same time that we gained the privilege of going barefoot, the honeybee started to patronize the yellow heads of the dandelions. And sometimes we barefooted too close to the gatherers of pollen and nectar. The result was a yelp on our part and a quick trip to see mother.

She checked the burning spot, often removing the stinger of the honeybee that had attacked us. After that she applied a paste of baking soda and water. The baking soda came out of the yellow Arm and Hammer box that she kept in the cupboard for baking, bee stings, and the brushing of one's teeth. The paste was held in place by a clean cloth secured with a piece of string from the ball that accumulated as a result of salvaging every "hunk of twine" that wandered into our home. It was before the magic of Band-Aids.

I suppose mother learned of the baking soda remedy from her mother, who learned it from her mother. Interesting enough, the chemistry behind it is valid. The honeybee injected an acid; the baking soda plus water makes a mild base which neutralizes the acid. I am not sure how much of the base got down to the formic acid under the skin, but we always felt better after mother ministered to us.

Later as I taught biology, I would ask my more advanced students to show me by the use of the microscope why the bee's stinger usually remains in the person or object stung.

In this exercise one must remove the stinger from a worker bee. Since the stingerless drones are loafing back at the hive, any busy bee will be a worker possessing a stinger. Either by using a tweezer and pulling at the terminal abdominal tissues, or by macerating (fancy word for mashing and separating) the entire abdomen on a microscopic slide, one can find the stinger.

If the stinger is cleaned up a bit and laid out on a slide, one has a fifty-fifty chance of solving the problem immediately. Coming out from opposite sides of the shank of the bee's stinger are several tiny barbs. They allow the stinger to enter the flesh, but they resist the retraction of it.

If the pupil cannot see the barbs, then it means they're lined up in the same vertical plane with the shaft and it will need to be rotated forty-five degrees so they lie in the same horizontal plane.

It is an interesting biological problem to solve, the discovery of why bee stingers tend to stay put once they have been put into action. It raises another interesting point. What happens to the now stingerless bee?

When the honeybee attempts to withdraw its stinger, the barbs hold it fast in the flesh. The bee escapes, leaving its stinger behind, plus some vital parts of his internal structures that are torn out. Result? The bee dies. So, if it is any consolation to the barefoot boy who got stung by a bee, his enemy will never sting again. Because of the loss of those abdominal parts, the bee will die.

When the hive, the honeybees' home, is disturbed, it is not a single bee that loses his life, but dozens of them usually make the sacrifice. I am sure that they do not realize the implications of their stinging, that it seals their own doom. But even if they did realize that it meant death, I believe they would do it. The social insects have strong drives that obligate them to protect the society to which they belong. They lay down their lives for the queen, for the larvae, for the honey, for their own right to engage in the food-gathering process.

Seldom do we hear in recent years of a Christian laying down his life for the gospel. It is true that in 1956 five brave missionaries who sought to bring salvation's good news to the Auca Indians of South America paid for their daring with their lives.

And history reveals others. John and Betty Stamm became Christian martyrs in China in 1934. Nameless ones died because of their relationship to Jesus Christ back in the first century AD, sometimes at the hands of Jews, sometimes at the whim of such political leaders as Nero, Emperor of Rome. In the seventh and eighth centuries Christians died at the hands of the followers of Muhammad. There was persecution again in the Middle Ages, during the Reformation period. Recently one hears scattered reports from Africa that some Christians suffered death rather than "reconverting" to tribal worship. But the "Stephens" of today are few and far between—at least in North America. Paul was ready to lay down his life for the gospel, but the volunteers in the 1970s are not exactly stumbling over one another to get in line for such a declaration.

One wonders why there are not more martyrs today than there were in the past? A book, *Martyrs Mirror,* contains accounts of many early

Anabaptists who gave their lives for what they believed, but we would be hard pressed to write a book about today's martyrs who died for their faith in Jesus Christ. If the blood of the martyrs is the seed of the church, it would seem that not much seed is being planted today. Such scarcity may bode real problems for the church of tomorrow.

There may be several reasons for our martyr famine today. Perhaps the level of tolerance in the world is higher. People are not so easily offended at the Christian witness. They are more broad-minded, more civilized. And undoubtedly this is true. Many "headhunters" and "cannibals" of yesterday have either been decimated by "Christian" explorers and settlers or they have become members of the establishment.

But there is another possible reason. Perhaps as Christians we are just not as ready to put our lives on the line. Perhaps the neat niches we have found ourselves in are too comfortable. Perhaps our comfort encourages us to dilute our religion until it is no longer offensive. Perhaps it is not just that the tolerance of the world's "headhunters" toward us has changed; perhaps as Christians we are more tolerant toward the "headhunters." And so we no longer speak up against the false religions of today. We make no waves, we rock no boats. We accept the cults, the Far East religions, the gurus of today, as providing methods of finding peace with oneself, one's fellowmen. We scarcely feel that such "isms" enable a person to find peace with God, but we remain quiet in our doubt.

When the honeybee attacks, when it defends, its life is given. Christians today seem much less aggressive, less positive, less anxious to upset the status quo. We are the gentle people. I know of only three people in my denomination (Mennonite) who could possibly come under the martyr category during the last fifty years.

Life seems more precious to us today. The stinger of the honeybee is fashioned to penetrate, to remain. It is as if nature designed it so that the honeybee attack would be guaranteed to be successful. Once the penetration is made, there can be no withdrawal. The formic acid will be released; the bee will have sacrificed himself for the welfare of the hive.

God gave us humans the power to think about the extent of our commitment. One feels that we are sometimes committed to "live" for Him, but not to die for Him.

Indeed all who desire to live a godly life in Christ Jesus will be persecuted. 2 Timothy 3:12.

10

Dangerous,
But
Necessary

Insects do not have an internal skeleton as humans do. Instead, their skeleton is on the outside of their body, a tough layer of tissue known as chitin. Periodically, as an insect grows, he must move out of his old skeleton because it has become too small for him. So the insect goes through the process of "molting." During this process his old outside skeleton splits, usually down the back, and he crawls out of his previous confining quarters.

Sometimes we find the final molt of the cicada nymph on the trunk of a tree near where he emerged from the ground. There it hangs, a thin brown shell, neatly slit down the back, the cast-off garment of the "seventeen year" locust. The former occupant is now busily engaged in insect orchestration among the leaves above. He holds his green-veined wings proudly over his inch-long body, whirring sounds arising from the vibrating membranes on his abdomen. His old brown suit is only an empty reminder of the past, of the time when he was nothing but a root-sucking nymph in the earth below.

In looking back, in tracing the molts, one could say of many insects, "Baby, you've come a long way." Beautiful butterflies arise from crawling wormlike larva that went through the process of molting, of casting off the old to make way for the new. To grow, to change, to live, insects must molt.

Now such animals that shed their exoskeleton may find themselves a bit handicapped as a result of that process. For example, consider the crayfish, who, believe it or not, are rather close relatives of the insects. They both belong to *Phylum Arthropoda,* a large grouping in the animal kingdom where the "joint legged" ones assemble.

The crayfish too sheds that outward armor. And when he does, the body beneath is at first very soft and easily damaged. When we were boys and caught such crayfish, we called them "softies." They were choice finds for they proved to be excellent bait for bass fishing. So, the softness of the arthropod's body after that molting is a price he pays for growth. It is a necessary change that he must accept. To do otherwise is to remain small.

As Christians we sometimes refuse to "molt." We are satisfied to do things as we did in the past. We witness the same way. We read the same books, talk with the same people, say the same things. For every day, we have a cliché.

And in so doing we limit our spiritual growth. We are confined, fenced in, imprisoned by our own safeguards. We feel comfortable with what we know protected us in the past. The past is our Maginot Line, but it can be outflanked. At the best, by refusing to change, we remain spiritual midgets because of our self-imposed limitations.

I know that spiritual molting is both a struggle and dangerous. An insect does not just "pop" out of its old skeleton. It would be more accurate to say that he "fights" his way out of it. And for a time he is more vulnerable than previously. Like the insect, like the crayfish, the Christian must accept that risk in order to grow.

If an insect had never molted himself, I suppose the first time he viewed the process, it would look like a pretty silly thing to do. But later he would find out that it was normal. If he refused to be normal, his insect life would be shortened, miniaturized.

Perhaps as a Christian I need to see change as a possibility for growth, not just leaving the security of my old limitations.

But grow in the grace and knowledge of our Lord and Savior Jesus Christ. 2 Peter 3:18.

11

Insect
Samsons

Sometimes we see interesting comparisons made between the strength of insects and the strength of man. We have made such comparisons in the chapter about "The First Astronaut" where we compared the flea's jumping ability to man's. There are other illustrations.

Experiments have been done which revealed a leaf beetle pulling a load some forty times its own weight. But a stag beetle did even better, pulling a load 120 times its own weight. The same beetle held a weight of seven ounces when suspended by its jaws.[1]

From such experiments we derive statements of comparison that make man look rather puny. For example, the stag beetle's display of strength would suggest that if man had proportional

1, Alexander and Elsie Klots, *1001 Questions Answered About Insects* (New York: Dodd, Mead and Co., 1961),pp. 50, 51.

strength according to his weight, he should be able to lift 10 tons or 20,000 pounds. Most of us do quite well lifting 100 pounds or 1/200 of what a "man-size beetle" could seemingly manage.

Man is actually not such a weakling, but a true understanding of why he isn't is a bit involved. The comparisons are usually made on a mass to mass relationship, and this is not fair. The drawback to making such direct comparisons is that the strength of a muscle is proportional to the area of a cross section of the muscle. As it grows in size its strength increases in proportion to the *square* of its linear (length) dimension, but the volume or weight increases as the *cube* of that linear dimension.[2] The strength does not increase proportionally with size. An animal three times the size of another will not be three times as strong. Simply put, it might be said like this: "You cannot divide the weight of a beetle into your weight and describe what load you should be able to lift or pull if you were all 'beetle.' "

But regardless of whether we understand the mathematics above, we would all acknowledge that insects are, weight for weight, quite strong compared to man.

Certain locusts have been known to fly continuously for nine hours. A scientist crossing the Mediterranean Sea from Algiers to Marseilles noticed a robber fly keeping pace with the steamer for an entire afternoon while the boat made a steady progress of fifteen miles per

---

2.*Ibid,* pp. 50, 51.

hour. The robber fly maintained the pace a few inches above the deck rail, never faltering, never landing for a rest.[3]

Frank E. Lutz in studying leaf-cutting ants examined their loads and found one carrying a leaf that exceeded its own weight by a factor of ten. She was carrying the leaf up a seventy-six percent grade at a rate of three feet per minute. Could we see ourselves trying something like that if our weight factor was only half of that for the ant?[4] For a 150-pound person this would mean carrying a 750-pound load. There would be a few strained muscles in our midst.

A caterpillar of the goat moth species escaped from under a bell jar which weighed half a pound and had a four-pound book resting on it to "guarantee" that the caterpillar could not lift it.[5]

A pair of sexton beetles have been known to roll a large dead rat several feet to a suitable spot for burial. The beetles lay on their backs, placed their legs against the carcass and shoved. And the rat moved.

What is the secret of the insect's strength? The number of muscles they possess is certainly one factor. Those muscles are extremely small and difficult to count, but all insect anatomists are convinced that they have many more than man possesses.

Another factor is the insect's ability to increase

---

3. Edwin Way Teale, *Grassroots Jungles* (New York: Dodd, Mead and Co., 1937)p. 75.

4. Frank E. Lutz, *A Lot of Insects* (New York City: G. P. Putman's Sons, 1941), p. 133.

5. *Ibid*, p. 285.

its oxygen consumption. A human being during excercise can increase his oxygen intake by nearly thirtyfold. An insect, say in flight, is able to increase it up to 100 times its normal rate.[6] This makes a difference since muscular contraction involves the use of oxygen.

We talk sometimes of "strong Christians," of "weak Christians." What is the secret of our strength? Is there some way that we can flesh out our spiritual muscles, flex them in the eyes of Satan so that he draws back, recognizing that he is no match for us? Is spiritual strength innate within us, some Christians "having it," some not?

The best advice I ever received as a Christian along this line came from an older brother in our fellowship who would occasionally "corner" me as a young lad in our church. After the service, he would find me, grasp my hand, and as he was shaking it with enthusiasm and love he would say, "Well, Robert, how are you getting along in your Christian life?"

After giving him my bulletin for the day, he would always offer the advice: "Well, just keep on praying and reading the Word."

Without question his advice was valid then and is dependable for today. The fasting and praying of Jesus surely strengthened Him for that wilderness experience. We are told that He often departed to a solitary place, there to pray. His Gethsemane praying surely prepared Him for Golgotha dying.

---

6. Klots and Klots, *op. cit.,* p. 51.

To search the Word is to find strength. The Bible contains a multitude of promises that buoys up the Christian, lifting him from despair, encouraging him, strengthening, providing new hope and confidence to face the problems, trials, and opportunities of this life.

There is another source of strength for the Christian, another source of fresh oxygen. It is according to the old saying, "There is strength in numbers." As a Christian who fellowships with other Christians, I can testify of that fact, of that strengthening, soul-filling oasis. In prayer meetings, in Sunday school classes, in worship services, I have found new tonic that can put fresh spring and strength into my Christian walk.

Through sharing and caring in such groups, I have found a type of involvement and support that builds me up. My fellow Christians' confidence in me, their love for me, gives me the strength to resist temptation. My concern for them, for their needs, sends me to my knees whether I am tired or not, there to wrestle with God for them like Jacob of old. And I arise a stronger person because of the sense of community I feel coming from such intercession. In turn they intercede for me. And with God it counts.

A single bee is of little concern to me. I can stand his sting. But a swarm of bees is a different matter. The poison of their combined injections could send me to a hospital, to my death. I respect the strength of numbers. Satan is forced to do the same. When the children of God combine their efforts and assail the gates of heaven, strength comes to push back the gates of hell. Satan is defeated.

I cannot fly like the robber fly; I cannot push like the sexton beetle; I cannot pull like the stag beetle; I cannot jump like the flea, but I can bury myself in God's Word, in prayer, in the fellowship of the believers—and strength will be there to meet the needs and problems of each day. Through these three media I can find the optimism, the faith, the encouragement that will enable me to rise Phoenixlike from the ashes of despair. Surely God is our refuge, a present help in time of trouble.

The Lord is my light and my salvation; whom shall I fear? The Lord is the stronghold of my life; of whom shall I be afraid? Psalm 27:1.

12

He Lives
But for
a Day

Some insects are named for the month in which they seem to flourish. The mayfly is a good example. But this delicate, gauzy winged insect is not to be confused or mixed in with the ordinary flies of the insect order, *Diptera*.

Mayflies belong to the order of *Ephemerida*. A rough translation of that Greek word is, "living but for a day." The adult mayfly that we see usually lives for only twenty-four hours as an adult. That brief life span is preceded in some species by four years of living in the water as a "wiggler," the larva of the mayfly. The larva is the life stage that follows the egg and comes before the adult stage.

Our adult mayfly is often found along streams in great numbers on a spring day, and is seen flittering and dancing about lights at night. Mayflies seem like such gay little insects, tiny triangular wings carrying them in ascending and descending columns of happiness. But the fragile little mayfly we see in flights of ecstasy today will be dead tomorrow. When we see the adult mayfly, we may be seeing him for only .07 of one percent of his total life. We are seeing the adult in action just before his death.

There is one key activity that must be completed that day. It is mating. Otherwise the species cannot continue. One of the last acts of the female during her brief twenty-four-hour life span as an adult is to lay her fertile eggs in a nearby stream. Some one to four years later, depending on the species, her offspring will emerge, crawl up on a twig or grass stem hanging into the water, shedding its skin for that primary molt. Within a short interval of time it will molt again, emerging as an adult mayfly, but only for one day of life.

If God gave me one day as an adult Christian, how would I spend it? The mayfly's life is not complete until mating has taken place and new mayflies are assured for the future. One wonders what priority a Christian places upon the act of assuring the production of other Christians?

I wonder how many Christians awake in the morning and say to their Creator, "Lord, if this is my last day on this earth, the only day remaining, let me during this twenty-four hours be used to win a soul to Christ, someone to continue His work here upon this earth. Let the kingdom continue."

I wonder what our priorities are? I wonder how many Christians greet the dawn without a single thought of priorities, of goals for the day?

And if we do set up goals, is God called in as a consultant, One who helps us to decide what will be our first, second, and third declaration of intent for the twenty-four hours before us?

One can walk across bridges and stroll beside streams where the spent bodies of mayflies and their previous molt cover the concrete and ground. It was their first day, their last day, their only day as an adult mayfly. They may be trodden under foot by man in death, but the Creator-centered priority of reproduction was fulfilled before death.

Has God not established such a priority within us, that of "reproducing" other Christians, winning persons to Him? If so, have we recognized that priority, or are we only flittering and dancing about the world?

We could learn something about priorities from the mayfly.

"We are not doing right. This day is a day of good news; if we are silent and wait until morning light, punishment will overtake us." 2 Kings 7:9.

13

Thirty Thousand Ommatidia

When the dime stores of the 1930s got in their "microscopes," I felt that I had to have one. They were over a dollar in price, but someway I procured the money, an immense sum for a teenage boy of that day. The exciting micro-world called me and I had to answer it. The advertisements on the microscope set box, the ballyhoo on the counter where they were displayed, promised me "hours of pleasure."

As usual, however, the advertisements were a bit in excess of the real thing. The bee's tongue, the fly's eye, the frayed cotton thread were not quite as spectacular under the cheap lens system as I had been led to believe by the pictures on the box. Only the salt crystals, tiny cubes, had much resemblance to the glories proclaimed. But it was a beginning, and I caught the "bug."

Later in high school, then in college and university, finally in teaching, I have been able to travel in that unknown world of smallness by magnifications of 100 times, 430 times, even 1,000 times.

Insects are so small that often magnification is needed to see the true beauty and complexity of their parts. The compound eye of the insect is an example.

Many insects have five eyes. There are three small ones, each known as an ocellus. Their purpose is not entirely understood, but they are sensitive to light and in some cases can perceive movement. In the early stages of an insect's life the ocelli are the only means of sight. They cannot, however, give a clear picture of an insect's surroundings.

The compound eyes are often large and bulbous, dominating an insect's head. When we have a dead insect, say a grasshopper, an interesting experiment with the microscope is to slice off a thin section of the outer portion of the eye with a sharp razor blade. I have had students do this, then place it under the low power objective of the microscope. This gives a magnification of 100 diameters. And then we can really see why it is called the compound eye!

The compound eye is made up of many tiny, separate optical units known as ommatidia, each with a six-sided lens and sensory cell. The lenses are neatly arranged, tightly packed on the compound eye surface, reminding one of the panels in a building with a geodesic dome-type roof. Each of these miniature hexagons function as a separate light receiver and together probably give the insect a mosaic view of his world.

The ommatidia, sometimes numbering 30,000 per compound eye, undoubtedly give the insect a good concept of movement, but are most likely rather poor at distinguishing detail. Their sharpness of vision probably is limited to a two- or three-foot range. It has been said that even the keen-eyed honeybee has a visual acuity equal only to 1/100 of that of man, while the fruit fly's drops to about one thousandth of ours. We keep saying "most likely" and "it has been said" because it's tough to get a grasshopper or honeybee to share exactly what he sees. And not many optometrists specialize in insect vision.

But one can say for certain that insects are rather nearsighted, without much ability to see detail. We recognize that a three-foot range of sharp perception for them might sound pretty good when we take into consideration their size, yet their vision is scarcely comparable to that of man, even when their smallness is taken into account.

To be nearsighted, farsighted, or to suffer from astigmatism certainly has its disadvantages. I am personally farsighted, which means that I wear glasses for reading. The nearsighted person wears glasses to correct for distant vision, while the person with astigmatism has his eyeglass lenses ground to correct for uneven curvature of the lens within the eye or the cornea surrounding the eye. But to be a nearsighted Christian certainly is worse than any of the physical handicaps mentioned above.

Bees and other insects have compensating senses to make up for their lack of visual acuity.

For example, the sense of smell in many insects is highly developed. But the shortsighted Christian has nothing to compensate him for his loss.

The nearsighted Christian cannot see God's long-range plan for his life. Romans 8:28, the verse which speaks to the fact that all things occurring in our lives will work out for good is not accepted. The unhappy event of today looms so large and so clearly in his vision that it blocks out tomorrow.

The nearsighted Christian is often judgmental. He judges not only God, but also his fellow Christians. Thus a spirit of criticism seems to dominate his evaluations. He looks at what he sees in the light of today. He wants quick results. He cannot look ahead for the long haul. He seeks the quick payoff not only in his own life, but also in the life of the other.

The picture that the insect gets of the world about him is probably pretty hazy. As suggested, those thousands of facets in the compound eye work independently one of another. And that accounts for the mosaic-like picture he receives, without the distinctive clarity, completeness, and distinguishing features of normal vision. Nearsighted Christians have a fuzzy, jumpy view of life. They have a tendency to see every event in isolation, not viewing it as a part of God's total plan.

A few water beetles come with bifocals as standard equipment. Their eyes have separate sections, one for viewing objects in the water, another for viewing things in the air when they are on the surface. God gave them a type of bifocals long before Benjamin Franklin invented them. The Creator knows His business.

Does God care about us, the way we "see" things as they come into our lives? Certainly He does! God does not want one of His children to be limited in his spiritual vision. He does not want us to be nearsighted like the insects, unable to look ahead, dissatisfied to let God fit present-day happenings into His total life plan for us.

Nor would God have us to be farsighted, so heavenly minded that we are no earthly good. He placed us on this earth for a purpose, and we have no business ignoring the world's needs about us as we stare off into the distance contemplating the blessings coming to us in heaven.

Neither would God have us suffer from spiritual astigmatism, seeing life in a distorted manner. God wants to have clear vision, sensing with vividness His presence and will in our total lives.

I know of no optometrist who is fitting insect glasses. But I know of a God who can accurately prescribe, grind, and fit corrective "lenses" for any visual difficulty a Christian might have.

The hearing ear and the seeing eye, the Lord has made them both. Proverbs 20:12.

14

The Achilles' Heel Of the Dragonfly

When we went fishing as boys and a dragonfly gracefully balanced on our fishing line, we were glad. To us it was a sign that we were going to get a "bite." When we were younger, the presence of a dragonfly was not such a happy occasion. We called them the "devil's darning needles," and the rumor circulated that they were equipped to sew up the mouth of any little boy who told a lie. It was before the days of women's liberation and girls were probably exempt from such stitching.

Actually, dragonflies are helpful to man, at least when they are adults. As nymphs (sort of an insect teenage stage) they live for several years in the water, and during that time they may feast on a minnow or so, with emphasis on the "so."

But as adults, when we see them skimming gracefully over the water, hovering delicately in one spot like some miniature helicopter, they usually are in quest of insects to quell their king-sized appetites. Among the speedier of the flying insects, some dragonflies can zip over the ponds at twenty-five miles per hour. To maintain that speed takes a lot of energy. And the dragonfly finds it by consuming his own body weight in insects every couple of hours. That's a lot of gnats and mosquitoes. If the sun is out, the dragonfly is usually on the prowl, making his appointed rounds, policing the pond or riverbank in quest of food.

The dragonfly is ideally equipped for both pursuing and escaping. His eyes dominate his anterior (front) end. Those large bulbous eyes in front stand out like two radar domes and are each set with perhaps 25,000 lenslike facets. Few moving objects escape his vision.

And if that is not enough, the dragonfly has another built in ability to complement both the position and quantity of those light receiving orbs. His head is attached to his body in such a way that he can swivel it about in almost a 360° circle.

With large eyes and mobile head the dragonfly can readily find his prey and skillfully avoid his enemies. It is difficult to approach a dragonfly without being spotted, for one comes into his vision range from almost any angle. So he patrols his river beat with seeming impunity from his enemies.

But he does have one weak spot in his observation setup. His view is clear, unobstructed to the front, to the sides, above, and below. However his long abdomen that trails behind blocks his view to the rear. It is his blind spot, his "Achilles' heel." To capture a dragonfly is not easy, but by taking advantage of that one blacked out area your chances are sharply increased.

I doubt if there is a Christian alive who does not have a weak spot, an "Achilles' heel." None of us, no matter how mature we are in the Lord's work, can afford to let our guard down for an instant. Satan surely knows that weak spot and is only waiting for a choice moment to move in and ruin our Christian testimony.

Many pastors have fallen, many elders strayed, many Sunday school teachers have been humbled because sin entered through that unprotected spot, a weak area that Satan discovered and upon which he capitalized.

A dragonfly does not know his visual weakness. As Christians we may know what our deficiency is. That knowledge should ring a warning bell when temptation comes. If my weakness is alcohol (and I believe the wise Christian will leave it totally alone), then I dare not taste it. If my area of shortcoming centers in that unruly member, the tongue, then I need to think twice before I speak once. If lust is my problem, then I need to be careful of what I read, the movies I see, the television I watch.

If the dragonfly knew his visual blind spot, he could compensate for it by body movements. If I as a Christian know my weakness, my limitation, then I can guard more carefully against the attacks of the evil one. I would not be proud of my weakness, but like the alcoholic who has become an alcoholic anonymous personage, I can learn to live with my weakness. I need not be captured from behind like the dragonfly.

Therefore let any one who thinks that he stands take heed lest he fall. 1 Corinthians 10:12.

15

"Unable to Fly,"
But
He Does

The expression, "As busy as a bee," is usually applied to the honeybee. It applies as well to the bumblebee, perhaps more so. A young honeybee does not begin his beehive duties until about two weeks old. The baby bumblebee begins his labors when he is only forty-eight hours old. Evidently child labor laws are nonexistent in the bumblebee world.

My experience with bumblebees is limited but memorable. The last occasion on which I renewed acquaintanceship was only several years ago, and of all places, in a graveyard. But I found the bumblebees there very much alive. In fact, they gave me new life, or at least unexpected movements.

It has been our custom to keep a small country cemetery mowed where some of my relatives are buried. That morning I was attending my business when I disturbed a nest of bumblebees under a fallen tombstone.

My first warning that I had been trespassing was my only one. It was to the point. I became aware of half-a-dozen or so burly bumblebees boiling the air about me. They landed, deftly inserted their stingers, injecting a drop of smarting formic acid and left. I also left the scene, eight or nine bumps miraculously appearing on my arms and shoulders.

Queen bumblebees are the only members of their particular tribe who winter over the cold season. In the spring they often set up housekeeping in abandoned mouse runs or other ready-made homes. Evidently a queen had decided that the fallen tombstone was a satisfactory place for rearing a family. My lumps were ample proof of her success.

Someone (sometimes attributed to Darwin) has said that the strength of England depends upon the number of old maids present in that country. The reasoning goes like this: "If there are many old maids in England, they will have many cats, since such ladies often keep pets as companions. The cats will catch field mice which frequently destroy bumblebee nests. This will mean that there will be more bumblebees which are needed to pollinate the red clover of England. The increased clover crop will feed a large number of beef cattle, and since roast beef gives strength to the men who man the English navy, it becomes very obvious as to the importance of having a suitable number of old maids in the British Isles."

The industriousness of the bumblebee is hard

to match. Not only do the young bumblebees begin working at an earlier age than the honeybees, but they put in longer hours. You will find bumblebees out working while honeybees are still sleeping in. Sometimes when nights are clear bumblebees work the whole night through. They are found at work collecting nectar and pollen in weather that keeps the honeybee at home toasting his bee toes in the warmth of the beehive and probably reading the *Bee Gazette* until the weather clears.

Bumblebees are workaholics. They don't know when to stop, literally working themselves to death. The typical bumblebee wears himself out in three to eight weeks. It is true that the honeybee may last no longer, but since the bumblebee puts in longer hours, his total work output is probably greater.

To strengthen the above point, the bumblebee actually performs under impossible working conditions. It can be proven from an aerodynamic standpoint that the bumblebee cannot fly. His wing area is not sufficient to support his bulky body in flight. The bumblebee doesn't know this and flies anyway. This is a beautiful example for any Christian carrying a heavy work load. God gives us the grace to "fly."

A Christian brother whom I greatly admired often quoted the old saying, "I would rather wear out than rust out." And he applied this especially to his Christian life. He found time to be most active in the work of the church in addition to carrying on a successful furniture repair business.

It was his habit, when occasion arose, to clean out his furniture truck and prepare it for the transportation of Sunday school pupils. Long before the bus ministries of today which are carried out by many large churches, Claude Leininger had a truck ministry going for his small church.

As a Sunday school superintendent in a large church, he was called to the same ministry in a mission Sunday school where he threw his whole heart and soul into the work of that small body of believers.

Shortly before he died I visited him in his home in Elkhart, Indiana. He was bedfast at the time, only semiconscious. I prayed with him, thanking God for his busy humming life. I found Christ as my personal Savior in the little mission church to which he had been called to serve.

There are many dancing, flitting insects in the world. The butterflies and moths, damselflies and dragonflies, the gnats and fruit flies seem to be content to live in a casual, relaxed manner. It is true that in their dancing-flitting activities they may be at work, but it is work done at a much slower pace than that of the bumblebee. He works as if possessed, as if the turning of the earth upon its axis depended upon his industriousness.

Driving, throbbing bumblebees have a hard time holding still. When I disturbed them in the cemetery, I doubt if they were on a coffee break. The ones who dive-bombed me undoubtedly were on guard duty. When I invaded their territory with my noisy lawn mower, they flew to the attack, performing well their assignment. For the remainder of that summer the grass grew tall around that particular section of the cemetery.

In the church today we sometimes hear grumbling about how some members of the "nest" do not carry their share of the load, that a few do all the work.

This may be true. Now to which group would we sooner belong—the slackers who avoid every assignment they can, or the workers who carry the load? Somehow I agree with my former Sunday school superintendent that wearing out is preferable to rusting out.

A rather trite saying, yet one that speaks volumes to the matter is, "Only one life, 'twill soon be past. Only what's done for Christ will last."

Christ's commending words, "Well done, good and faithful servant; you have been faithful over a little, I will set you over much; enter into the joy of your master," would appear to me to be adequate payment for any life-giving service we render to the One who did so much for us.

Then he (Jesus) said to his disciples, "The harvest is plentiful, but the laborers are few; pray therefore the Lord of the harvest to send out laborers into his harvest." Matthew 9:37, 38.

16

The
Organ
Builders

We live in an age of automation, of cybernetics, of computers. We have each had both pleasant and unpleasant experiences with this last fellow, the computer who has invaded our everyday life. One is amazed at the way the computer "memorizes" vast quantities of information and then sorts it out for instant recall. But one is also disturbed by the "bullheadedness" of the computer that refuses to change its mind and bills us for payments already made. We recognize man's responsibility as a programmer cannot be denied, yet we often think of a computer as being almost human, as thinking. We congratulate the computer; we condemn the computer.

Insect thinking is computer like. They seem programmed to go through a set of actions in a definite pattern. We commonly refer to such "thinking" as doing things by instinct. It is as if the insect's head contains a tiny tape recorder with all action programmed upon it. The reel starts and the insect goes through the actions scheduled upon the unwinding tape.

We might take the mud dauber wasp as an example. One species from this group, the organ pipe mud dauber, has frequently chosen a small utility building on our one-acre "farm" as a place to raise their young. We call this structure to the back of our lot, "the shed." It is a six by eight building that was constructed to relieve the garage of accumulated lawn mowers and bicycles.

Sometimes the children have come flying out of the shed, bitterly complaining of the "wasps." And the wasps upon occasion have given them a bad time, circling threateningly about their heads. Actually none of us has ever been stung by these particular mud dauber wasps that have used the interior of the shed as a shelter for their tubelike nurseries. When the wasps get excited because of our attempted removal of the lawn mower, we usually give them five minutes or so to simmer down (or leave) and have no trouble getting out our machine. Seldom have we found it necessary to get violent with them.

The mud dauber wasps that built on our property must have transported their clay pellets at least a quarter of a mile, either from the creek or a neighbor's farm pond. I know of no other source of clay that would be closer. Since each cell constructed takes an estimated twenty-five to thirty loads of clay, one can see that the project is no small affair.

The mud dauber's computer causes the insect to complete the following pattern. First a site must be chosen for home building. Then a suitable mud source must be found. This is followed by the twenty five or so trips necessary for the completion of the cell that is being plastered on the interior walls of the selected barn, shed, or garage. Each clay pellet is carefully cemented to the previous material gathered. Since in the case of the organ pipe mud dauber the individual containers are often constructed side by side, occasionally one rising higher than the other, we gave them the name we did because the completed structures resemble organ pipes. Once the clay cell is completed, several spiders are captured, paralyzed, and placed in the earthen home. An egg is laid in the cell during the spider collection excursions. Finally the opening is sealed. The paralyzed spiders will provide a fresh food supply for the mud dauber larva after it emerges from the egg.

The sealing of the cell with the final dab of mud is the end of the computer tape for this wasp. The tape must now be rewound before the process can be repeated. The mud dauber does not think as we do, his every action being programmed. Every step must be done right the first time. There is no going back to straighten anything out. The tape runs relentlessly. There is no reviewing button to push, no fast forward. It is a rigid formula that the wasp follows. This fellow, like all other insects, is an automation. He does not reason; he simply jumps through the hoops that heredity places in front of him.

Perhaps some Christians would like that sort of an existence. Perhaps they would like to live the Christian life without thinking, never having to make decisions, just proceeding from womb to tomb under some predestined plan.

But God has arranged for us to think, to reason, a much higher form of mental activity than the mud dauber possesses. That higher level has its drawbacks. With it we can make mistakes, can hurt ourselves and others through wrong decisions. And at times there are tons of frustration weighing upon us as we do our deliberating.

Why didn't God program us like He did the insects? At the risk of second-guessing God, I think there are several reasons that we can reasonably mention. Obedience that comes as a result of demand, praise that is given because a certain button is punched, worship that evolves only as a result of reminders, is hardly the level of obedience, praise, and worship that is worthy of a God our size.

God could have made us puppets, marionettes dangling from strings under His control, but He had a better plan. God wanted us to develop, to become persons in our own right, yet under His direction. It is not a paradox. It is entirely possible for us to become through our choices what He wants us to be.

How is this possible? How can a Christian be a free person and yet be exactly where and what God wants him to be in thought and deed?

They say, "Christ is the answer," and He is. When we let that Man possess us, dominate us, then our choices, our decisions are made under

His direction. Surely one cannot object when he is programmed by the Master Programmer. When we are Jesus-oriented, and genuinely Christ-centered then our life unreels under divine guidance.

The words of the previous paragraph are acceptable to the Christian. We buy them even as the sinner envies them. And yet we who acknowledge the truth of those words still wonder about the mechanics of this miracle. How does it actually come about?

Every Christian is conscious of what it means to let Christ come into his life. We know that this occurs when we accept God's redemption plan, recognize Christ as Redeemer and *Lord*. Sometimes we forget the "Lord" part. Each of us finds himself, however, either wanting to program his own life, or having certain uncertainties about what He wants us to do. We fear that the tape is getting tangled, that it is blank, that God might have us running at "fast forward" instead of "normal."

When such feelings come, it would seem that we need a larger dose of reassuring comfort. And this is found through a deeper infilling of the Holy Spirit. This happening is sometimes referred to as the baptism of the Holy Spirit, a new anointing, a fresh outpouring of God's Spirit, or a Pentecostal experience. The terminology is not as important as the happening.

Surely God does not want us to live our lives either in mechanical, robotlike manner, or as trembling, questioning, and doubting people. The Holy Spirit is waiting to add His stamp of approval, His note of authority to God's plan for us in Christ Jesus.

That's why there is a triune Godhead.

When the Spirit of truth comes, he will guide you into all the truth; for he will not speak on his own authority, but whatever he hears he will speak, and he will declare to you the things that are to come. He will glorify me, for he will take what is mine and declare it to you. John 16:13, 14.

17

Saucer
Of
Honey

Many of us have been involved at one time or another in the game of charades. At parties we may have acted out an event, perhaps a Bible story, without the use of words. It was a test of our acting ability, a taxing of our pantomime skills so that people could see by our expression and movement the message we wanted to convey.

Charades are interesting, a bit frustrating, and we emerge from them with a keener appreciation of our sense of speech.

The experience of Helen Keller, her inability to see or hear, further illustrates the problems that arise when one cannot use the tongue of one person to set in vibration the eardrum of another and through that common yet complex process communicate by speech and hearing. It is true that we remember little of what we hear, but for the daily run-of-the-mill communication needs, speech is hard to beat and a good ear is most valuable.

Insect sounds may be produced by vibrating membranes,wing action, or the contact of an insect's body against some part of its environment. Most insect sounds are courting sounds and many of *Class Insecta* are silent members.

Some insects have ears for receiving sounds. The ear may be located on the insect's leg, abdomen, or chest! But on many insects we have no evidence of ears. So, not all insects "talk," not all insects "listen." Then how do they communicate?

Undoubtedly the antennae of an insect are used in communication. Some entomologists believe that these "feeler" organs help an insect to engage in sensations beyond that of touch. Most insect scientists agree that the perception of chemical vapors is received by these antennae.

But insect communication may be a good deal more involved and sophisticated than what we have been led to believe when we see several ants crossing antennae. We were made quite aware of this by the work of Dr. Karl von Frisch of Austria who has done a remarkable piece of work at translating bee language into a form of "English" that we can understand. He found that bees use a type of charade communication. The "listeners" who are actually "viewers" seemingly have no trouble getting the message from the charade actors.

Dr. Frisch's technique for breaking the bee's communication code was as follows. He placed saucers of honey at varying distances and in different directions from the hive. He marked visiting scout bees who dropped in at his honey saucers with tiny dots of paint and studied them as they returned to the hive. By using red light to illuminate the inside of the hive he was able to do his viewing without disturbing the hive activities. As the scouts returned to the hive with a load of their "saucer honey" they went into a little "bee dance." By a series of movements inside the hive, by using circles and figure eight formations, by varying such movements both in speed and with slight changes in the pattern of the dance, the scouts were able to communicate to the bees in the hive the good fortune they had in finding a source of food. Other bees became excited, exited from the hive and moved in the correct direction and distance to the food source.

It took thousands of tests by the Austrian scientist to understand what the different bee waltzes meant, but his findings were verified by others who examined his data and validated it by their own observations. The good news was given directly by the scout bees to other members of the hive, and the honey saucers were quickly emptied.

I am convinced that Christians should be "dancing." I think we have good news for both sinners and Christians. But can they understand our language? Can they break the code we speak?

Christians have a way of using some pretty sanctified terms. And to the sinner it may become a strange language. Our message may be lost amidst the semantical confusion of Christian clichés

Educators, and I am one, have been accused of speaking a certain jargon, a peculiar educational gobbledygook that turns off lay people interested in school policies and happenings. As educators, our language may be devised because of basic insecurities. We love to talk in our flowery language of five and six syllables. It helps us to convince ourselves that we are a special breed. Perhaps every profession is guilty of this, hiding behind words, portly terminology that we use to guard either our secrets or our ignorance.

A Christian's words may be shorter than the educators, but equally strange to the non Christian. A story I heard, perhaps made up, is told about a sinner's answer to a Christian's eager attempt at witnessing. To the Christian's question of, "Did you know that Jesus saves?" the sinner innocently replied, "No, I didn't know that Jesus saves. What does He save? S & H green stamps?"

Bee language is relatively simple, and the bees understand what the returning scout is saying. Are sinners hearing us? And more, are they understanding the message?

What do the following words mean to a nonchurchgoer: salvation, justification, redemption, sanctification, predestination, consecration, regeneration, purification, atonement, born again, lost, saved, and similar terms that we Christians throw around loosely? One wonders at times if we ourselves understand what they mean.

Sharing our Christian faith is sometimes difficult enough to do in the "hive," but how do we do it outside the church? Certainly one thing we need to be sure of is that our "bee dance" accurately reflects the facts. If a scout bee finds nectar one mile east of the hive and gives the bee movements that says the good crop of clover is two miles west, then he creates more problems than he solves. His dance does not live up to the facts of the case.

If my life says one thing and my speech another, I am a confusing person to the sinner and he will have trouble interpreting my message.

As a Christian I should be following several rules in my attempts to communicate successfully to the world. I must say things simply, in the language of the people with whom I converse. I must begin where they are at, not where I am at. The witness must be natural, not forced.

Second, what I am saying must not be contradicted by what I am. It is one thing to speak of the fruit of the Spirit, but I negate such language if my own life proves that I am proud instead of meek, that I am not at peace with my fellowmen, that I am not living a temperate life. The old saying, "Your life speaks so loud that I cannot hear what you are saying," was never more true.

And lastly, I must be sure that the message is for the right purpose. Some Christians notch sinners on their conversion belts like savages hanging scalps on their war lances. A scout bee does not return to the hive saying, "Look at the load I've gathered! What a wonderful bee I am!" A scout bee comes back with a message of success, but saying, "Come share with me. Taste of that which I have found." Perhaps such scouting bees should be thought of as "praising bees."

As Christians, one of our greatest means of communicating to the world of that which we have found, one of our greatest ways to issue an invitation for sinners to try Jesus, is for that world and that sinner to see us living a simple, happy Christian life, one in which we are rejoicing in the Lord.

A specialized honeybee waltz can only be interpreted by another honeybee or someone of the Dr. von Frisch caliber. As Christians we need to develop a "waltz" that the world can quickly recognize, that can be easily translated, losing nothing of significance in the translation.

The world may not understand what it means to be saved, to have been redeemed through the precious blood of Jesus Christ. But they should be able to see by my happy Christian life that I have found the "saucer of honey." Let me first point them, first lead them to my sweet Savior. After we have had the experience of drinking from that fountain that never shall run dry, then we can struggle with the language.

To speak the language is not as important as having had the experience.

One of the two who heard John speak, and followed him, was Andrew, Simon Peter's brother. He first found his brother Simon, and said to him, "We have found the Messiah," (which means Christ). He brought him to Jesus. John 1:40-42.

18

The Sand Thrower

What insect excavates a funnel trap in sand for capturing unwary ants and proceeds to cause sand slides to keep his intended victim from escaping the sloping pit walls?

If you do not know the answer, you need to toil through the next three paragraphs as a penalty for your ignorance.

Listen carefully, for we need to distinguish between several insects before we arrive at the one we have described. Accuracy may be tedious, but it is not a sin.

The ant lion and the damselfly are easily confused. Both of them also resemble dragonflies in general. Now damselflies and dragonflies belong to the same order of insects, *Odonata,* and are rather easy to keep apart. The dragonfly is somewhat heavily bodied and holds his four wings out horizontally while the damselfly rests with her wings together above her more slender body.

The easiest way to separate the damselfly from ant lion is to check for the presence of short, clubbed antennae. If they are present, it is an ant lion; damselflies have no antennae. Our ant lion belongs to an entirely different order of insects than dragonflies and damselflies, namely *Neuroptera.*

So in one short lesson you have now become an authority on identifying dragonflies, damselflies, and ant lions.

Additional facts that we will throw in at no extra charge to help us keep these fellows straight are that dragonflies and damselflies frequent streams and ponds while the ant lion which resembles the damselfly so closely does not mind the drier habitats. If we ranked the three according to flying ability, the dragonfly would come in first, the ant lion a poor third. But the ant lion is still the hero of this chapter.

The name "ant lion" is descriptive of the larva, not the adult. Mother ant lion lays her eggs on sandy, loose soil, not in the water. When the larvae hatch out, they proceed to dig a funnel-shaped pit in the sandy soil and bury themselves at the bottom, nothing protruding but the head. But that's enough. The ant lion larva has a pair of massive, formidable jaws that resemble the curved scimitars of an Oriental warrior from an earlier time period.

Without reading further, you can now see the plans of the ant lion larva. A strolling ant tumbles down the side of the funnel. At the bottom are the waiting jaws of the "lion." And if the ant catches itself part way down and begins to scramble up the sloping sides, the ant lion at the bottom has another trick up its insect sleeve. With a snap of his head, the ant lion hurls a few sand granules above the ant which is clawing his way up. The tossed sand sets up a miniature sand slide and the frightened, doomed ant drifts downward to the waiting jaws below. A bit horrifying but still pretty neat, at least from the ant lion's viewpoint.

How detailed a trap the ant lion sets! How persistent his efforts to stop the escape of a single ant which comes close to his abode!

To set a trap for the sinner, to impede his chance to escape, may sound like poor Christian ethics. But I wonder. Jesus told His disciples that He would make them fishers of men. A fisherman does not just casually stand beside the stream, hoping the fish will jump into his creel. No indeed. The fishermen I know, by "hook or by crook" seek to capture the wary fish. By bait, by varied techniques, they try to make it almost impossible for the fish to refuse what is offered.

I wonder if as Christians we might not be a bit too gentle, a bit too willing just to let things happen? We speak in this book about the need not to build up walls, not to offend, but we must not fail to see the other side. Unfortunately, aggressiveness is often not the Christian's bag.

The ant lion plans to capture ants. He builds a device to bring him into contact with ants. And when they are there in his bailiwick, he seeks to make them his own.

I realize that some might challenge my analogy. Some might say that the Christian should not use trickery to get people close so that a witness can be given, that the sinner should be left free to make his own decision.

This is true; the sinner needs to make his own choice. Salvation is by the free will of man. But I wonder if the other thesis needs to be invalid, the idea of the Christian having designs upon the sinner, making plans for his capture, setting traps for him.

Some of us came to Christ during the revival meeting era. That was the trap that caught us, be it the hellfire and damnation sermon or the lovely prodigal son story. Invitation song after invitation song was sung. Those were the grains of sand that were tossed at us to impede our escape. And finally we were caught, not by the jaws of an ant lion, but by the all-encompassing love of Jesus Christ, the wooing of the Holy Spirit that prevented our fleeing from the Master's call. Was that bad? I was caught in the revival meeting trap and I am glad. Praise God it was set for me.

Jesus spoke in Luke 14:28-32 of the need for planning if a city was to be built, if a war was to be waged. I wonder if the same is not true of our Christian witness. We need to build some "sand funnels," we need to toss a few "grains of sand."

There are other "traps" besides the revival meeting. There is the Sunday school trap, the small-group Bible study trap, the weekend retreat trap, and so on. They are traps to trip up the sinner, to slow him down, to get him to stop and look at himself.

If the word "trap" bothers us, let us call them "devices." The world has many, many devices, creative advertisements to capture people, their money, their desires. I believe it is time for Christians to do some creative planning to plot aggressive strategy. We make all sorts of plans in our business world to capture customers. It is time that we make such plans for capturing sinners. Some Christians are already doing this, using ant lion techniques. Fine, we should join them.

Anyone can live a Christian life devoid of conscious, directed witness planning. And in the process, it is surely possible that some neighbor or friend may be captured for Christ through such low key, unconscious letting of one's light shine from gentle elevations. Lovely. Praise God for the silent, come-as-you-will, happy-go-lucky type of witness. Anything is more than nothing.

But somehow I believe that the ant lion's planned method of contact and capture would be more profitable. I vote for an open season on sinners.

To the Jews I (Apostle Paul) became as a Jew, in order to win Jews; to those under the law I became as one under the law—though not being myself under the law—that I might win those under the law. To those outside the law I became as one outside the law—not being without law toward God but under the law of Christ—that I might win those outside the law. To the weak I became weak, that I might win the weak. I have become all things to all men, that I might by all means save some. 1 Corinthians 9:20-22.

19

The
Unliberated
Male

Among the larger insects you might meet is the giant water bug. And you will most likely capture him under a streetlight, not in the water!

This large, flat bug ranges from one to two inches in length. Some tropical species reach four inches in size. This qualifies him as one of the giants of the insect world. And he is not a harmless giant. His front legs are designed for grasping his meal, be it other aquatic insects, minnows, small fish, or even a water snake. Water bugs are able to conquer larger animals because they inject a poison where they bite that cuts their victim down to water bug size. Their sucking mouth parts then enable them to siphon body fluids from the animal they have captured.

Perhaps turnabout is fair play. A giant water bug not only eats, but it is eaten. The Chinese consider them a delicacy and one can imagine that quantities of them could make a very crunchy meal. I have had these insects brought in during insect collection time, but I have never had either the desire or nerve to check on their palatability.

It is true, however, that insects are a staple item of diet in some countries. Among other insects eaten are crickets, grasshoppers, and insect grubs of various kinds . Grilled termite grubs are a delicacy in Africa. WASPS (White-Anglo-Saxon-Protestants) squirm at the thought of including such creatures in our diet, but I'm not sure what our basic objection actually is to partaking of them. John the Baptist of Jesus' time seemed to do quite well on a diet of locusts and honey.

Sometimes you will find the giant water bug called the electric light bug. This is because in summer months, being a strong flier, he likes to take off from his lake resort and visit the city. Unlike us, who prefer the lake in the summer, he seems to like to take in the bright lights of the city nearby. And if in the process of visiting the corner streetlight, he touches down on land, then he is easily captured. He is a skillful swimmer, a strong flier, but a lumbering, awkward pedestrian.

The giant water bug should be picked up with care, since his bite can be painful. But like some other insects, he may try to fool you also with his "play dead" act.

One is not likely to see this insect in the water in spite of their size because of their strange way of resting. They "hang" downward from the water surface, only the tip of their abdomen projecting into the air above. Their trachea (breath-

105

ing tubes in the abdomen) thus have contact with the air. In this manner they are able to rest comfortably in safety with very little giant water bug showing.

The most interesting point to me about this insect is what happens at egg-laying time. When the female is ready to lay her eggs, she looks around for a suitable object upon which to deposit them. More often than not, she finds a male of her species standing by. She grasps the male and proceeds to fasten her forthcoming eggs securely upon his back. She does this despite his squirming and generally uncooperative action.

Insects lay their eggs in a favorable spot for hatching, typically in or on a suitable supply of food for their emerging children. Many insect eggs, however, never hatch because they are eaten by hungry enemies. But here is an insect that almost guarantees her eggs will hatch. Few water inhabitants will attack the giant water bug with the idea of feasting on eggs cemented to his back. The carrier of those eggs is too tough a fellow to tackle. It would be like you or me challenging the heavyweight boxing champion of the world to a fifteen-round match.

The male giant water bug plays the role of nursemaid to the developing eggs. He is the mobile baby buggy, the portable nursery for the giant water bugs that are to be. It is not a typical male role among the insects. Even in the social insects, it is the female worker that does all the baby rearing, the caring for the young larvae. Drones, male honeybees, are considered lazy. In fact, when the word "drone" is applied to a human, it is usually in a derogatory fashion, suggesting that he is only a parasite on society, a nonproducer, a non-contributer.

Those of us who have raised families or are in the process of doing so, if we are honest with ourselves, will admit that the male image in the family is sometimes lacking. The children see little of it. We have a tendency as husbands and fathers to relegate child rearing to the wife, to the mother. A day at the office, in the factory, on the farm is thought to be our contribution. We are the breadwinners; let the women rear the children. We even argue that women are best equipped for doing this, since they tend to possess quiet inner strength and patience as well as innate teaching abilities.

They say that a child's picture of his heavenly Father may spring from what he sees and learns of his earthly father. "A child who senses only a mother's care may get shortchanged in regard to how he pictures his heavenly Father as a loving, caring personage." The male giant water bug is committed to the early responsibility of its young developing within the eggs on his back. Where he goes, they go. I am not sure how much of paternal instinct he has by nature, perhaps none, but like-it-or-not, he carries the load after the eggs are laid.

From this we are not trying to say that the roles need to be reversed in our families. But I wonder if fathers should not be seen a bit more about the home, changing diapers, rocking their children, reading them stories, putting them to bed. Raising children is not only for the female.

As parents we are interested in our children being raised in the admonition and nurture of the Lord. It is interesting that Ephesians 6:4 which expresses this previous thought is addressed to fathers.

We want our children to receive a good picture of God. If it is true that a child's concept of a heavenly Father may be derived from the model he observes in his earthly father, then we in this family role have a frightening responsibility.

Perhaps the female giant water bug is saying to the male when she plasters her emerging eggs upon his back, "Here, take them. Up until now the responsibility has been basically mine. Now it's time that you did something." We may be putting untruthful words into an insect's mouth, but surely there is a point here for us men to take seriously.

In our Christian homes, where an order is described as 1 Corinthians 11, we men have a responsibility, a serious one of providing leadership. That leadership certainly doesn't mean that we abdicate our own child rearing responsibilities. Perhaps in too many homes the women must rise in protest and say to a negligent, unseeing husband-father, "Do something. Help me. I can't bear this load alone."

And we males should humbly hear that cry, accepting those father responsibilities without the squirming, uncooperative reactions of the male giant water bug that does his duty only when forced into it.

Likewise, you husbands, live considerately with

your wives, bestowing honor on the woman as the weaker sex, since you are joint heirs of the grace of life, in order that your prayers may not be hindered. 1 Peter 3:7.

20

The Orange Traveler

In Pacific Grove, California, it is illegal to disturb or kill a butterfly! This sounds strange to us, since we don't feel that the life of an insect is that precious. We have swatted flies and mosquitoes with glee without feeling that we are violating the law. True, butterflies are in a different category, yet laws for their protection seem to be carrying things a bit far. But it is so. The city has the ordinance and it is enforced.

The "butterfly trees" of Pacific Grove have become tourist attractions. Each fall the monarch butterfly returns to this area, landing in the tall Monterey pines of the coast. There they cluster in such large numbers (perhaps 2,000,000 in all) that the green-needled trees appear a brown-orange in color. They remain on the trees during the winter, fluttering about only briefly if a warm day appears.

The "butterfly trees" were first discovered at

the beginning of the century. These monarchs seemingly have decided to winter in California instead of Florida. Like the regular return of the swallows to Capistrano, the butterflies can be counted on to arrive in Pacific Grove, California, by the last Saturday in October. On that day a special celebration and parade are held in their honor.

The migration of birds has long been an object of study, interest, and amazement. Arctic terns nest in the tundra far north of the Arctic Circle during the summer. In the fall they migrate over open seas to the far reaches of South America. Their round trip is some 22,000 miles. They complete it without maps or compasses.

The monarch butterfly is not so ambitious, but for an insect traveler of such fragility it is remarkable. A technique has been devised for successful marking the wings of butterflies so that we can keep track of them much as we do for birds by banding them. Dr. F. A. Urquhart of Toronto, Canada, has pioneered in this area. Monarchs, and remember the adult may only live nine months, have been known to fly from Massachusetts to Florida.

Having been alerted by radio announcements, I have watched through binoculars the monarchs pass over our home in northern Indiana on other migration routes. Their flight, I observed, is one of gentle flying. There are no speedsters among them. Seemingly they husband their strength for the long journey before them.

Various theories have been proposed on how birds are able to navigate with such skill year after year. Explanations sometimes given are based on the birds' ability to respond to the earth's magnetic field, the earth's rotation, or star position. Yet each theory has its limitations. We are not certain.

But how do the much more simplified monarchs make it, probably a once in a lifetime affair. From where comes their sense of direction, from whence comes their sustaining strength for such a long and adventuresome flight?

One must remember that the monarch butterfly weighs only .4 gram or 1/70 of an ounce. They have been known to fly from Ontario to Texas within a month, averaging over thirty miles per day. That such delicate creatures can complete such a grueling trip is almost incomprehensible to us.

Several interesting parallels for the Christian come out of our study of the monarch butterfly. And I think we can find a more definite answer to our questions in this area than we can for the ones proposed above concerning our *Lepidoptera* friends.

The two questions we might ask are: How do I find my way as I move pilgrimlike through this earth, and from whence do I receive the strength to make that pilgrimage? Although we do not migrate like the monarch, we do want to move at God's command. And although we do not fragilely fly through the air high above, nevertheless, we do struggle through this vale of tears below. Leading and strengthening is essential for us.

Surely our compass is the Holy Spirit, accurate, totally reliable. Jesus promised that the Spirit would come to guide us into all truth. *The Living Bible* paraphrases it this way, "When the Holy Spirit, who is truth, comes, he shall guide you into all truth, for he will not be presenting his own ideas, but will be passing on to you what he has heard" (John 16:13). The Holy Spirit is our hot line to God.

And I believe it is so. To me this simply means that we must first commit our lives to God, that this must be followed by a complete trust in Him. And now He speaks to us, guides us, directs us in our "migration" through the Word, through the counsel of God's people, the church of today. The believers are a discerning body, some with special gifts of discernment given through the Holy Spirit, and I believe that God wants us to make use of the counsel of those so gifted. The Holy Spirit gives guidance in the making of decisions by God's people and follows it with His own confirmation.

We can only theorize how birds and monarchs migrate, how they receive their sense of direction. There should be no theorizing as to the source of the Christian's direction. Scattered throughout Jesus' farewell words to His disciples in John 14 to 17 are a number of references to the Holy Spirit's role in guiding, comforting, glorifying, and I would add, "providing migration instructions."

And as to the strength for my Christian flight? It is of God. David, a man who did much "migrating" because of Saul said it ever so simply:

"The Lord is the strength of my life" (Psalm 27:1, KJV). David clung to God's promises.

It seems impossible that the delicate wings of the monarch could carry him those many miles to his destination. And at times it may seem impossible for us as Christians to stand under the burdens the Lord allows to be placed upon us. But He allows nothing to come to us that we are not able to bear. Jesus traveled the same route I must travel. He blazed the way through Gethsemane to Calvary. And I should be able to follow.

Yes, God provides both the guidance and the strength for my fragile flight through this world. He does it through prayer, through the church, through the presence of Christ in my life, through the comforting, directing Holy Spirit, through His precious Word. I am not certain to which "Pacific Grove" He would send me, but I am confident that He knows the way, that He provides the strength. If the monarch can make it, so can I.

I will instruct you and teach you the way you should go; I will counsel you with my eye upon you. Psalm 32:8.

21

A First
In Mobile
Homes

What insect builds his own private home around himself, lives in it for nearly a year, always carrying that house with him? Most amateur entomologists will not know the answer to the question.

If we had asked what mollusk (shelled animal) does the same, we would have been flooded with answers such as oyster, clam, snail, and the like. If we had asked what reptile lives in his own house, we would receive "turtle" answers. If we had inquired about colonies of insects that build homes, then we would have been pointing to the order *Hymenoptera* where the bees, hornets, and wasps belong. But even here, such house builders do not carry their homes with them. So to ask what insect not only builds his single home, but also carries it with him for a particular portion of his life, could stump a few of us.

The caddis fly is the answer to our puzzler. His

solitary housing development takes place only in the larva stage. The adult caddis fly is a rather drab, nondescript insect, more interested in walking than flying. It is related to the moths and butterflies, but different enough to be placed in a separate insect order, *Trichoptera*.

The adult caddis fly is sometimes called the water moth. It is usually more active at night and is frequently found near water. During the day the adult usually rests, holding his wings roof-like over his body as the locusts. He is not brilliantly colored like some butterflies and has no spectacular eyespots on his wings like some moths. He is usually colored a shade of brown or gray, sometimes black. Certainly the color does not call attention to himself. And it is just as well, since he has little going for him defensively. The caddis fly has no stinger, no protective disagreeable odor, and is a weak flier. His best protection is to sit still, hoping to remain unnoticed. Evidently such survival tactics succeed for there are over 4,450 species of caddis flies in the world today.

The female lays her eggs in the water and the larvae hatch into an aquatic environment. They come equipped with abdominal-placed gills which enable them to extract oxygen from the water. The front of the larva is brown and heavily armored, protected by a tough layer of chitin, a shell-like covering comparable to the outer layer of the crayfish. But the abdomen is white and soft. One can imagine the danger to which this subjects the larva. On the brown stoney or muddy bed of the stream, white would be a contrasting color that would help its enemies to spot it. And the softness of that exposed body part would mean that the predator need experience little difficulty in whacking off a healthy, easily digestible section of caddis fly larva steak.

So what is the caddis fly larva to do? Ah, very interesting!

The larva immediately begins to gather construction material. According to the species this may be tiny grains of sand, minute pieces of wood, or small pebbles. From the mouth parts a silklike glue is emitted that soon hardens after contact with the water. The sand grains or other building materials are neatly and skillfully cemented together about the soft body parts until a tube is formed to both disguise and protect the caddis fly larva. Then he anchors himself in his own portable little tunnel. His rear is now protected by "cement blocks" or "two-by-fours," his front has his own personal chitin armor, and his legs are exposed for mobility. He is a veritable tank in motion, ingeniously constructed and directed long before General Patton arrived on the scene.

As the larva matures, the mobile home is enlarged, even rebuilt. The rear of the tube is closed by a silken plate with a hole through it to allow fresh water to circulate so the gills may take out the needed oxygen for the occupant to "breathe." This is his home for most of the year that his life cycle takes.

Within this home, or a newly constructed one, the larva goes into the pupa stage, a period of rest

117

that just precedes adulthood. He then escapes from his aquatic home and emerges as the drab, dull-colored, rather uninteresting adult. Certainly his "teenage years" in the water are the most exciting.

I think we differ from the caddis fly in several respects concerning this armor business. As Christians, we need it *all* during our lives. I doubt if there is a time when we who have enrolled in the ranks as soldiers of Jesus Christ dare take off our armor. And we certainly need that *complete* armor.

Paul speaks in Ephesians 6 of this armor. What part would we scorn? Paul calls us to put on the breastplate of righteousness, the helmet of salvation, the strong belt of truth, to have our feet shod with the gospel of peace. In our hands we are to hold the shield of faith, the sword of the Spirit.

Our Lord asks us to take this armor for both offense and defense. In so doing we shall build a wall about us like the caddis fly larva, a wall that will protect us from the fiery darts of Satan. But it will also be a castle from which we dare sally forth to do battle with the powers of evil.

I doubt if there is a Christian today who is "over armored." Each of us needs to accept from God every bit of help He offers, every piece of that armor. And like the caddis fly larva we should constantly be examining that armor, keeping it in good repair, affirming its need for both ourselves and our fellow warriors.

It is only through using God's armor that we shall be able to reach that state of maturity where we can be classified as adult Christians, trained soldiers in God's army of righteousness.

Therefore take the whole armor of God, that you may be able to withstand in the evil day, and having done all, to stand. Ephesians 6:13.

22

A
Knight in
Dotted Armor

We called them ladybugs, although I'm sure that half of them were male. But it was and is an honored identification—the insect supposedly was named after Our Lady, the Virgin Mary.

Again, I am bothered by poor nomenclature. The true bugs belong to *Order Hemiptera*. The ladybug is really a beetle and belongs to *Order Coleoptera*. We may be confused about her exact and correct classification, but we are not confused about her being a good insect.

Like most people, I learned early that this was an insect to respect. And I practiced what all children practiced. When we found one of these small orange beetles with black spots, we placed it on our open palm and recited,

> "Ladybug, ladybug, fly away home.
> Your house is on fire and your children
> will all burn."

There are variations on that last phrase, "your children alone" or "your children all gone," but it didn't seem to matter which version you said. The ladybug always got the message. She climbed out of your palm to the tip of a finger and obediently flew away. As children we supposed she flew to her burning home and then rescued her offspring. More than likely she flew to a plant that contained some scale insects or aphids, there to devour them in large numbers.

Many of us have heard how the ladybird beetle (a bit better terminology than "ladybug") saved the citrus crop of California. The establishment of citrus fruit groves in California was accomplished in the 1800s. By 1850 fortunes were being amassed in the orange groves of the Golden State. And then a fearful visitor arrived, the cottony-cushion scale insect from Australia.

This insect quickly spread throughout the state, attacking the citrus trees, wiping them out or crippling their production. The scale insect sucks the sap from any plant upon which they are located. The eggs are laid in small patches of cotton-like material upon the plant and it is from the appearance of these white patches that the name cottony-cushion scale is derived.

The salvation of the citrus fruit industry came about through our ladybird beetle. It was noticed that these attractively colored beetles kept scale insects in check in Australia. They were imported to the United States and immediately proceeded to do the same job here. Today they are gathered at hibernation times, stored, and actually sold by the quart or gallon to those who appreciate this natural way to keep harmful insects in check.

Interestingly, this insect had been accepted as man's friend even previous to this. This neat little quarter-inch-in-diameter fellow, looking almost round from above, but flat from beneath, is nearly a perfect hemisphere. There are over 3,000 known species of this insect, most of them spotted black on a red, orange, or yellow background. Black on orange is the common variety we encountered as children.

Most people are not familiar with the black sheep of the family *Coccinellidae* where the ladybird beetles are slotted. The genus *Epilachna* (a smaller division than the family grouping) contains four North American species that are plant feeders. All the other continental members of this large ladybird beetle family are feeders on injurious pests—they are "meat eaters." Among the four black sheep are found the squash beetle and Mexican bean beetle. Both of these fellows are definitely pests. I suppose that the raisers of beans and the growers of squash do not have the love and tolerance for the ladybird beetles that most of us have. Such a farmer, especially if he had suffered crop loss because of one of these two rogues, might have a tendency to forget nearly 3,000 other "good guys" in the ladybird family. Is that fair to be prejudiced against 99.9% of a grouping because less than .1% of the membership gives man a bad time? It may not be fair, but it is done. When one is hurt by a single person, he often strikes out blindly against others. His prejudice becomes set, frozen. A bean grower whose crop has been damaged by the

Mexican bean beetle is much more likely to classify this family *Coccinellidae* (ladybird beetles) as villains, not heroes.

How easily we stumble over the mistakes of a few and as a result write off the good of many. The church has always suffered from the fact that a few in the name of religion have destroyed and torn down, have weakened or diluted, what others in the name of Christ sought to build up. Ananias and Sapphira may have been the first hypocrites in the church but they were not the last.

Most of us know of hardened sinners, sometimes former Christians who have had some bitter experience with the church, perhaps been grieved or offended by a brother in the fellowship. And the result is that through the error of one or two the entire Christian church has been condemned. Blanket judgments should not be based on a single experience. But they are.

Every Christian needs to walk with fear and trembling. A mistake on our part can push a nonbeliever further into his shell —can cause a fellow Christian to slip, to fall, to lose out in his Christian experience. Our zeal sometimes consumes us and we are too bold. Our shyness sometimes silences us and we are too timid. Again, to walk the knife-edge of obedience to the Holy Spirit's leading is a difficult task. Let us consider an area where we can either bring glory to God or we can hinder His cause.

In the Christian church today the charismatic movement has had its bright spots, its dark spots. Undoubtedly under a fresh outpouring of the

Holy Spirit we have seen God manifest Himself through new gifts to His people. We have seen people empowered as on the day of Pentecost, equipped for a much more intense and higher plane of living.

And we have seen people also who bear counterfeit gifts of the Holy Spirit. These gifts are not real. They are not genuine. They may be of Satan. Examples are few, but they are there. Having seen such counterfeit gifts, seen them with their cheapness and crassness, there is the temptation for the disappointed viewer to dismiss all the evidence of the charismatic movement as being false. And this is foolish.

If I am hurt by accepting a counterfeit ten-dollar bill, it does not mean that I stop using money. I simply become more careful in handling and accepting money in general.

The destructiveness of the Mexican bean beetle does not cancel out the worth of the other ladybird beetles. Their near relatives saved the citrus fruit industry of California. As a Christian I must not be discouraged by the damage caused by a few casual, careless Christians. Instead I remember the millions of Christians who have lived for Him and produced the true fruit of the Spirit.

I want to pray for the few Mexican bean beetle Christians around me. I want to praise God for the multitude of ladybird beetle Christians that are functioning fantastically in God's kingdom.

Beloved, do not believe every spirit, but test the spirits to see whether they are of God; for many false prophets have gone out into the world. By this you know the Spirit of God: every spirit which confesses that Jesus Christ has come in the flesh is of God, and every spirit which does not confess Jesus is not of God. 1 John 4:1-3a.

23

The
Dying
Caterpillar

Upon occasion I have observed caterpillars that are nearly covered with tiny white cocoons. When I was young and knew everything, I was sure these were eggs of the caterpillar being carried papoose style upon their mother. And if someone would have asked me how those "eggs" got there, I am sure that some explanation would have come spinning off the top of my shallow thinking head to answer the person who questioned my diagnosis.

But since my youth, I've learned a few things. The cocoon-like structures being carried by mama or papa caterpillar had nothing to do with their own reproduction. Caterpillars do not mate. Nor would the ones that I saw carrying their white "spools of thread" ever mature. Every caterpillar I saw with such a load was a dying caterpillar. Much of his internal tissue had been ravished by the quiet inhabitants of the egglike cocoons.

What had happened to my caterpillar friend in the past? He had received a "hypodermic injection" from a female wasp. It might have been the militant noctuid parasite wasp or another of similar breed. The hypodermic injection was not a shot to cure the caterpillar of some ailment. To the contrary, it was a death sentence.

The "hypodermic needle" was the ovipositor of the female. She needed a place to deposit her eggs. Like most insects she did not plan to stick around and care for her little ones. So she sought a place where they might be comfortably housed and fed. And she found it in the caterpillar. By piercing the caterpillar's "skin" she was able to deposit dozens of her eggs inside his body. The caterpillar might protest, but it was to no avail. Yet the worst was yet to come.

As the eggs of the wasp hatch out into larvae inside the caterpillar's body, they are in the midst of their food supply. They proceed to eat the fresh, living tissue of the caterpillar, feeding often on the blood and fat cells. It may be gruesome, but it is life. As the old advertisement by the tobacco company said, "Nature in the raw is seldomly mild." Survival of the fittest, the law of the jungle, prevails in the insect world also.

When the larvae of the wasp are mature, they emerge from the caterpillar's body, spin their cocoons, and add insult to injury by taking a free ride on the outside of their dying host. It is not enough to almost eat him alive on the inside, but after boring out and spinning those minute cocoons, they insist that his last act be one of giving them a farewell roller coaster ride to the spot where he decides to crawl off and die.

Unfortunately as Christians we sometimes allow ourselves to be exploited by parasites. We let Satan place in our minds, in our hearts, in our lives, ideas that will slowly consume us. Notice I say "let Satan." Here is a sharp, significant difference between the caterpillar and us. The caterpillar had nothing to say about whether he wished to be consumed by the larvae within.

We have something to say about it. When Satan comes to us with his cunning, attractive ideas, we do not have to listen. We have a right to refuse to be so injected.

For example, when the Father of Lies comes to us, suggesting that we should be informed about the evil around us, that a knowledge of pornography is a good and healthy thing for this reason, we do not have to buy his sales' talk. If we do, we may be infected and "eaten up inside" by this evil. If it does not consume us, it will weaken us. We'll never be the Christian we could've been had we refused to let Satan invade us in this way.

Lust is a larva that grows rapidly within us, continually making new demands as it increases in size. Flower flies such as *Syrphus Americanus* lay a single egg in an aphid. That ravenous larva consumes the entire interior of the aphid until only a hollow shell is left. And so it can be when Satan is allowed to deposit within us a single idea, however innocuous it may seem at the moment. Upon fruition it may devour our very Christian experience.

Is alcohol such a parasite? We recognize that alcoholism may be a disease, that a chemically imbalanced body may have little chance to fight it off. And yet none of us need to be parasitized by this destroyer. When Satan comes to us as an angel of light, seeking to deceive the elect of God, we must command him in the name of Jesus Christ to depart from us. And he must leave. The alcohol egg need never be laid within us.

A caterpillar once parasitized is doomed. How we rejoice that the Christian has other options. We need not let depression, hate, envy, jealousy, and pride gnaw away at the inside of us. We need not let these offspring of Satan have free rides at our expense. It is possible for the Christian to have victory through Christ over these innoculations by the devil.

A Christian who recognizes that Satan has successfully implanted within his own life that which is not of God can be delivered. But he must want that deliverance.

There is no hope for the caterpillar, but there is every hope for each of us. Insects in their simple lives cannot comprehend their problems. They cannot escape the consumption within. As Christians we can both comprehend and escape. One must be thankful that the parallel between parasitism in the insect and in the Christian is not complete. We praise God for the difference.

Submit yourselves therefore to God. Resist the devil and he will flee from you. James 4:7.

And He [Jesus] appointed twelve, to be with him, and to be sent out to preach and have authority to cast out demons. Mark 3:14, 15

24

Tougher
Than the
Dinosaur

The woolly mammoth, a saber-toothed tiger, the dinosaur are all examples of magnificent animals which once roamed this earth, but today are no more. Biological historians attempt to theorize why they became extinct. Did global changes in our climate cause their decline? Could the rise of the mammals have brought about the downfall of the dinosaur? Did the mountain building period in the earth's history cause the drainage of vast swamplands, the rise of new plants in a new environment which proved unsuitable for some of these forms of life? What global catastrophe occurred back there before written history that contributed to the death of these monster-masters of the past?

Perhaps man will never know for certain, but whatever the cause, the saber-toothed tiger, the dinosaur, the woolly mammoth, and other forms of life could not make the adaptation to the changing world in which they lived. And because they could not adapt, they passed into oblivion.

It is interesting that we find fossilized remains of cockroaches that were contemporaries of the saber-toothed tiger, the dinosaur, and the woolly mammoth. They are similar to the cockroaches that we have today. How amazing that this small pest survived in a changing world that eliminated the fierce giants we have named! One wonders why.

Again, our insect subject is not one of our favorite six-leggers. Few people love the cockroach although some scientists respect them. The cockroach has been used in basic studies of animal behavior, nutrition, and metabolism. They have been used also in cancer research. Studies indicate that they are among our brighter insects, one of the few that can be taught to run a maze.

But no matter how we flatter the cockroach, few people are willing to change their own feelings of strong distaste for this fleet invader of kitchens and restaurants.

Being poor had its disadvantages, but I would never have become familiar with this member of the insect world if it would not have been for our poverty during the Depression Years. There is some blessing in being born on the wrong side of the railroad tracks.

My earliest recollections of the cockroach comes from boyhood memories of a rented home into which we moved at Elkhart, Indiana. I remember going to the kitchen, snapping on the light, and seeing the speeding brown spots on the kitchen linoleum move helter-skelter to the shelter of the walls where they could slip under the baseboard.

When we moved into a rented house where cockroaches lived, Mother always quickly began her campaign against them. By keeping her kitchen spotlessly clean, covering all food, and using roach powders generously, she would win the cockroach battle. But for a time it made for lively living and one always kept a sharp watch for any revival of the population.

Mother had a saying, "One need not be ashamed of getting cockroaches but one should be ashamed of keeping them." And it is true that they may be brought unawares to your home from the grocery store and take up housekeeping in your kitchen, close to a source of food and water. But no one needs to live with the uninvited guests on a permanent basis.

The question we wish to look at is this: How did the cockroach survive countless centuries when the much larger animals failed to make it?

Their small size could be a part of the answer. A cockroach can hide more easily from his enemies than a dinosaur. Their bodies are extremely flat and they excel at slipping behind and under the woodwork. Among the insects they are the 100-yard-dash athletes, extremely fast.

Both the front and rear of their bodies are well equipped with appendages for sensing that danger is near. Antennae on the front of insects are sensing organs, thought to pick up either odor or heat. Tiny taillike structures at the rear of the cockroach are sensitive to wind currents.

The abdominal nerve cords that carry impulses to their legs are among the largest in the insect world. So the cockroach is well equipped for sensing danger and responding to it.

Some insects produce chemical substances that influence the behavior of the opposite sex. Female cockroaches produce a sex odor that brings male suitors running. No opportunity seemingly is missed for reproduction. Every female cockroach is almost guaranteed to become an egg layer, certainly one of the reasons why they have been able to maintain their species these many years. The female is one of the few insects that "cares" for her eggs once they are laid. She carries them in a little purselike package and waits until they are about to be hatched before depositing them in a crack in the floor. Migrating female cockroaches have been observed carrying those packets of eggs as they move to new quarters.

Cockroaches do not mind moving from the grocery store to your home. One fertile female is all that is needed to set up shop under the kitchen stove, producing in short order a colony in your residence. Cockroaches adapt to any home where they find food, moisture, and darkness. Since none of our homes are without those three qualifications, every home is a potential site for cockroach infestation.

So, since he is fleet of foot, alert to danger, skillful at evasion, maintains an active sex life, and willing to adapt to new surroundings, the cockroach has survived. His smallness is no handicap.

If the earth stands, will Christians last for hundreds of centuries? We have not yet reached our 2,000-year anniversary. If we survive, what will be the secret of our survival?

The church of Christ will not fall. This is a straight prediction from the Founder Himself. Her survival, however, can be hindered, her growth retarded, her outreach reduced. The cockroach may teach us something about successful survival.

As Christians, are we sensitive to the dangers about us? Can we move away from them? Do we recognize that at times retreat is the better part of valor? Perhaps "affluence" is the Christian's greatest danger today. In times of prosperity it is easy to forget the Lord. It would be interesting to check with fellow Christians what they consider our greatest danger to be in today's world and how we can best survive that danger.

The cockroach survives because of reproduction—one might almost say insistent, cleverly planned reproduction. Christians also must be reproducing other Christians, winning others to the Lord, being fruitful in Him, becoming fishers of men. How attractive are our lives to sinners about us? If the survival of Christianity depends upon each Christian winning another have I already made my contribution? Have I met my quota?

Do we care for our young in the Lord, the babes in Christ, as well as the cockroach watches after her eggs? Young Christians in the church need the care and concern of mature Christians. Do we give it to them?

134

How quickly can we move for the Lord, take advantage of a situation into which the Christian church should be moving, and become active in that movement? We know our intelligence quotient, but do we know our agility quotient? Are we slightly retarded in the latter, moving out for the Lord only when He practically kicks us into the action? The cockroach reacts rapidly to a situation, moving out with flickering feet. One senses that the church at times remains immobile, resting upon past accomplishments, or waiting until she feels that her chance for success is 99 percent or better.

Am I willing to migrate for Christ? This refers to more than simply making a move in a local situation. It may mean moving under the direction of the Lord to an entirely new, perhaps unfavorable locale. It is thought that cockroaches came to the United States on the slave ships of the 1700 and 1800s, moving from the security of the old world to the unknown of the new. I am pleased to see Christians today move out to new areas of witness, sometimes at great sacrifice. Like Paul, set apart by God, they travel to the Corinths, Lystras, and Philippis of today. There they invade a community, set up housekeeping, propagate the faith, and work at winning souls to the Master.

No, the cockroach is not a pleasant fellow, and none of us cares to live in a house inhabited by them. But they have survived much longer than some larger animals and we can learn from them some techniques for the successful survival of Christianity today.

Paul, an apostle of Christ Jesus . . . to Timothy. .
. . I am reminded of your sincere faith, a faith that
dwelt first in your grandmother Lois and your
mother Eunice and now, I am sure, dwells in you.
Hence I remind you to rekindle the gift of God that
is within you through the laying on of my hands;
for God did not give us a spirit of timidity but a
spirit of power, and love and self-control.

Do not be ashamed then of testifying to our Lord.
2 Timothy 1:1, 2, 5-8.

25

The Need to Struggle

Our family has planted carrots in our garden for two reasons. We like them and we like the black swallowtail butterfly. The black swallowtail has a preference for carrot tops when it comes to finding a suitable spot on which to deposit her eggs. So, it has always been a nice arrangement: we prefer what grows below the ground; they prefer what grows above the ground. We eat the orange carrots; the larvae which hatch from the swallowtail eggs are quite content to feed on the green foliage above.

And we like to bring the fat, developed larvae into the house, put them into a quart mason jar with some carrot tops. Then we can watch the larvae enter the chrysalis stage. It is intriguing to observe a larva spin a little silken girdle upon which to suspend himself, then split out of his larva skin and almost magic-like transfer itself from a mobile worm to a stationary, unmoving chrysalis. It is not impossible also to be present when the adult butterfly emerges to become the black swallowtail, all lovely spotted with yellow and blue, along with a bit of red.

And frequently we locate the large, papery cocoon of the cecropia moth, the largest of the American moths. The cocoons are noticeable in the fall and winter when the leaves have left the trees and shrubs. In the spring we bring them into the house, and if we are around at just the right moment, we watch this beautiful moth emerge with its spectacular crescent markings on each wing. Each wing is also bordered by bands of browns, ivories, and reddish orange.

What a remarkable transformation takes place when that dull pupa develops into a beautiful, active, adult butterfly.

When the butterfly emerges, damp with soft and flabby wings, one might be tempted to rush for the Kleenex box, to administer some help, to play the spanking, drying physician-nurse role in the delivery room at a large hospital. Don't. "Newly born" butterflies move to a place on a twig or branch where they can hang upside down. One dare not set them aright; they know what they're doing. They need space and time to inflate those baglike wings.

By slowly moving those wings, blood is pumped into the wings which are made up of two membranes. The blood separates the membranes which are prevented from swelling like balloons by tiny joining, supporting "rods" which allow the two wing membranes to separate a bit, but not too much.

Moths must struggle too from their cocoon in a similar manner. That very struggle is an essential part of their life cycle. To help them, to insist on lightening their burden, is actually to hinder them. Their private Gethsemane must be endured by them alone.

As parents we often find it painful to watch the growing process of our children. We remember some of our own hurts and struggles, and we would like to spare our children such "suffering." And frequently today we are better able to help them than our parents were to help us. These are affluent times. We can look back to the time when we were children, note where we are today, and declare with the psalmist that the reins have fallen to us in pleasant places. Because of our present solvency and our past experience, we often want to help our children over the rough spots. Such help can be dangerous.

Adults are inclined to forget the value of their own struggles. The difficult spots over which we moved, the problems from which we extricated ourselves, the depressions that we rose above, all helped to strengthen us. Like the moth, like the butterfly, we needed the struggling, the pumping to inflate our spiritual wings so that we could fly.

We needed to "dry off" naturally. We were still "wet behind the ears" and we needed to realize it the hard way. No one could tell us. We needed to grow up, to seize opportunities, to make mistakes, to recover, to learn from them. In that process we suffered, but by that suffering we grew. The saying, "Experience teaches a hard school, but fools will learn in no other," may not be flattering, but it fit us. And certainly it enforced and reenforced our learning.

We are not saying that children do not need help from parents. What we are saying is that the wise parent will come to the rescue of the child at the proper time. If an insect has become trapped in a sticky substance, he may need a helping hand to survive. But if the insect is going through a vital life process essential for normal development so that he may mature as an adult, then we do him no service by trying to circumvent that particular life stage.

A wise parent will prepare his children by example, precept, and training so that they can stand alone so they can advance successfully through the difficult teenage period of life.

That wise parent will know when to say, "Let me help you," and when to stand back and pray that God's Holy Spirit will enable his struggling children to emerge from the fire as a purified vessel, with wings strong enough to fly, now fit for the Master's use.

> Humble yourselves therefore under the mighty hand of God, that in due time he may exalt you. Cast all your anxieties on him, for he cares about you. . . . And after you have suffered a little while, the God of all grace, who has called you to his eternal glory in Christ, will himself restore, establish and strengthen you. 1 Peter 5:6, 7, 10.

26

Seventeen Years as a Teenage Insect

When we landscaped our one-acre suburban lot, the gentleman on the bulldozer suggested that he push over the small wild black cherry sapling growing in the front yard-to-be. Thinking of the young boys we had, their coming days of tree climbing desire, the possibility of a tire swing hanging from the limbs above, I said "No." And I have always been glad that I did.

The tree climbing boys developed; the tire swinging girls came along. The tree was a bit of a burden because of the clothes staining ability of its fruit, but it more than paid for its trouble when it introduced the children to the Rip Van Winkle of the insect world, the cicada.

We found the light brown empty shells fastened securely to the bark of the wild black cherry. They represented the final molt of the cicada nymph after it emerged from the ground. And he may well have been a subterranean dweller for seventeen years. That would make him a Methusaleh among the insects. Since there are over 800 species of cicadas in this world, I am not sure if the ones the boys and I saw were from the seventeen-year variety, but I would like to think that they were. A new brood of the seventeen-year locust emerges every year in this area while the thirteen-year locust (another common U.S. variety) is found further south.

For seventeen years that cicada lived as a nymph, an immature form of the insect. In the soil, unseen by man, he was content to molt, to slowly grow, sucking away contently at the root juices below the surface of the ground.

But when that seventeenth spring comes, ah, then it is a different story. Now the cicada nymph has reached the length of a fat inch. He laboriously constructs a tunnel upward and emerges in early summer, greeting the light of day for the first time in seventeen years. It is then that he works his way to my wild black cherry. In some cases he cannot wait to get to that nearest upright object, be it tree or telephone pole, to make that final molt, but emerges as an adult between tunnel exit and waiting tree.

What mysterious hormone triggers him off so that he knows this is the spring, this is the day to make his debut? His brothers and sisters seem to have that same hormone for they usually make it at the same time, within twenty-four hours of one another. We don't know what activating device rings the alarm clock for the cicadas. It is like a second birth for him, a new world of light and warmth. It reminds us of the conversation that

Jesus had with Nicodemus in John 3.

Whatever the hormone, whatever the clock, the brood is awakened on schedule. They find their way to a tree that may or may not have been there seventeen years ago. That final molt, that last shedding of their teenage garments, seems to qualify them as adults. Soon there will be mating. The female will slit the tree twigs and insert her eggs. The eggs will hatch, and the tiny cicada nymphs will drop "miles" to the ground. They are so light, however, that air currents buoy them up and they arrive safely to disappear into the soil for another seventeen-year stretch.

Our Pilgrim forefathers saw a brood of these insects emerging and thought of the biblical plague of locusts told about in the Book of Exodus. And there on our Eastern coast they wrongly named this insect from *Order Homoptera*. True locusts belong in *Order Orthoptera* along with the grasshoppers and crickets.

In spite of the "W" vein marking found on the wings, the cicadas are not a harbinger of war. They are annoyingly noisy. In fact their abdominal vibrating membranes are among the highest, if not at the top of decibel ratings among insects. Perhaps their long silence entitles them to sound off. But the poor female is silent. Only the male has the ability to arouse the neighborhood with song.

Our noisy friend is immature for seventeen years. Some beetles beat that record but it is still outstanding. For over a decade and a half the locust remains hidden, sucking away babylike on root juices.

The Apostle Paul worried about those whom he first brought to the glorious light of the gospel. He felt some of them were not maturing, content too long to remain as children, as milk feeders. In Hebrews 5 he urges them to become teachers of others instead of remaining forever as pupils. He suggests that they get off their milk diet and start eating meat, holding out that such a change in diet is normal. Evidently the Hebrews to whom Paul wrote were nymph-Christians, ground dwellers, root suckers.

The seventeen years a cicada remains in the ground are easy years. Tree root sap is nearby. He simply slurps it up, fattens himself, occasionally molts, living the "life of Riley." It is a period of contented, gurgling babyhood. Are there Christians like that today? There were in Paul's time. These Christians seek the easy route, remaining in the crib, bottle fed or having a pacifier popped into their gaping mouths by the preacher or an overindulgent Sunday school teacher.

In the life of Jesus, maturation came at an early age. At twelve, according to Luke 2, He felt the need to be about His Father's business. It separated Him from His parents, keeping Him all night at the Temple asking and answering questions of the wise ones. He got involved at an early age.

Perhaps some Christians are destined to be immature forever. If so, then the church needs to nourish them. But we dare not make such a blanket judgment and decision for all baby Christians. Some immature Christians are immature because they never had an opportunity to develop and the brotherhood is at fault for not providing the chance they needed to try their wings. Closely related to this, perhaps even being responsible for it, is the unwillingness of some mature Christians to lay down their established positions, to step back, and to let someone else step in.

Perhaps some pastors are themselves only milk feeders and know of no other diet to prescribe to those in the church nursery.

Perhaps some infant Christians need the "Holy Spirit fullness hormone" to energize them into making that final nymph-molt.

Whatever the reason, would to God that all sleeping Christians would awaken in their earthen tunnels, sense God's call to maturity, and then move into that stage where they stand up as adults, fit soldiers of the cross.

For though by this time you ought to be teachers, you need some one to teach you again the first principles of God's word. You need milk, not solid food; for every one who lives on milk is unskilled in the word of righteousness, for he is a child. But solid food is for the mature, for those who have their faculties trained by practice to distinguish good from evil. Hebrews 5:12-14.

27

The
Tail
Lighters

When the lightning bugs (fireflies) were abundant in the summer, we neighborhood children scurried around the community yards collecting them. With one swoop of a hand we captured them one by one as they betrayed their exact location with a beautiful flash of yellow light. And we put them in glass jars, fascinated and pleased by the amount of light they produced when half-a-dozen of them decided to flip their switches on at the same time.

Sometimes we were a bit hard on our captured insects. We held them in our hands until the abdomen lighted, then pinched off the glowing section. That part continued to glow for some time. Since it was a bit sticky after our amputation, we could fasten it to a finger. And so they became our glowing rings, entomological toys created by the poor.

By the way, our friends are neither bugs nor

flies. They do not belong to the true bugs, *Order Hemitera*, nor to the flies, *Order Diptera*. Actually they are beetles, belonging to *Order Coleoptera*. It is another case of where poor naming sticks.

As children we had no idea why the lightning bugs flashed, probably thinking that it was a method of finding their way or searching for food. But actually, as is well known today, they were seeking mates. Males cruise about, advertising their presence and interest in matrimony by intermittent flashings. Females who are interested respond and arrangements are made for further acquaintanceship.

There is enough difference between the flashing signals so that one variety of firefly is not rushed into seeking a mate from a different strain, one not on his particular branch of the family tree. Since there are more than sixty varieties of this insect in the United States, such timing must be a very accurate affair.

The simplest explanation given for the firefly's ability to make "fire" is that the chemical substance in its body known as luciferin is oxidized (united with oxygen) and the glow is the after effect of that oxidation.

Industry also through oxidation, or by other methods, is capable of producing light but with nowhere near the almost 100 percent efficiency of this beaming fellow. We do well to convert 8 percent of the energy passing through the filament of an incandescent bulb into light energy. We do somewhat better with the fluorescent lamp where the amount is raised to 15 percent. It is still a long way from the 100 percent efficiency of the firefly. Nature is hard to beat.

In tropical countries fireflies have actually been used to light the way through the jungle. Collected in jars in large quantities, some of the insects are always in the process of lighting up and a portable, living lamp is the result. Recently I have read how biochemists in this country are studying bioluminescence and in their quest for fireflies are paying school children for collecting them. What we did for fun has become a small business venture for others.

Christians also give off a light—or should. And it also should be for "attracting" purposes. This is made clear in Matthew 5:16. However, there is a basic difference between the attracting reason for the firefly and for our own. The firefly's motives are quite selfish—the male seeking to be the center of attraction, and his counterpart's responding for her own personal reasons.

The light which the Christian flashes as described in Matthew 5:16 is to call people to God. It is to glorify Him. To make certain that other people are attracted to God and not to us is most important.

A man in a drunken stupor hailed Dwight L. Moody on a Chicago Street one day, it is said, and identified himself as one of Moody's converts. Dryly, and undoubtedly with both sadness and confession, Moody replied, "You look like one of *my* converts." Moody was not in the business of soul winning to glorify Moody. He lit up for God, not for Moody.

To live the Christian life prosperously, successfully, attractively and to be able honestly to transfer any praise that comes to us to the Lord is not only important—it is difficult. It is so easy to accept the winsomeness that may be found in our lives as a personal asset, owned and cultivated by ourselves. Yet when a person praises us for what we are doing, the opportunity is always there to transfer that praise over to the One to whom it rightly belongs. How can we make this transfer from man to God without having it undeservedly stick to ourselves?

First we need to be sure that we recognize the source of our talents. They are God given. If Christ is Lord of our life, then they are not our own. What we have belongs to Him and the One who sent Him into this world to claim us.

We will need to be specific in this transfer. When we are praised, we will want to be audible on the matter. It may necessitate verbalizing like this at the time when praise or thanks come our way: "I praise God that He used me in that instance," or "Let's thank God for that."

When God uses us, when we manage to light up for Him, we should be thankful to Him, but also remember our many power failures, our blackouts. After all, because of our own short circuiting, most of us are rather inefficient lights for the Lord. Too much of the energy passing through is wasted in producing heat—the heat of arguments, of defending ourselves, of glorifying ourselves. What percent of our expended energy results in bringing glory to God? The firefly's light shows nearly a 100 percent usage of that energy, but ours is more comparable to a gaslight where only 3 percent of the energy is converted into light. We do not too often become cities sitting upon hills, giving light to all about us.

Is there a scarcity of hills upon which to position ourselves? Do we selfishly or with false humility carry bushel basket complexes which causes us to hide our lights? Have we a Sunday religion and as a result eliminate 85 percent of the week as being unimportant for light shedding? The fireflies I know work seven days a week.

The quiet, beautiful glow of the fireflies on a July night in our yard is a beautiful sight. But I want it to remind me of more than childhood games. I know that in spite of the beauty attached to the firefly's glow, it is a selfish glow. I want it to be a constant reminder of my need to glow, not for personal satisfaction, but so that my light may glorify my Creator.

You are the light of the world. A city set on a hill cannot be hid. Nor do men light a lamp and put it under a bushel, but on a stand, and it gives light to all in the house. Let your light so shine before men, that they may see your good works and give glory to your Father who is in heaven. Matthew 5:14-16.

28

Reproduction
Without
The Male

In visiting a local store I renewed acquaintanceship with a lady who had formerly attended
our church and been an active member of it. But
for several years now she had not attended, having voluntarily withdrawn from our fellowship, a
keen source of disappointment to the remaining
members.

At our store meeting I expressed some of that
disappointment and invited her to return to the
church. She gave me this reason for her
withdrawal: "I never could quite believe all the
doctrines of the Mennonites and that is why I
left."

I asked her which of our doctrines bothered
her, expecting her to name such a one as
"nonresistance" or the "prayer veiling."

Instead she said, "I never could accept the idea
of the virgin birth of Jesus. After all, nature itself
proves that this is impossible. You don't have

puppies without a father dog, kittens without a tomcat, calves without a bull."

I found a piece of paper and wrote on it the word, "parthenogenesis," and asked her if she would look up this word, hoping that it might help her to realize that not all living things reproduce by what seems to be the conventional method, male fertilizing the female, the embryo developing as a result of that fertilization.

I am not certain at what age I myself learned the truth about reproduction among animals and humans. I do distinctly remember that I carried for some time in my mind the "information" that babies came to families in the doctor's little black bag.

Back in the days when the physician still made house calls, it was always an important time when the doctor came to our home. We were awed with his knowledge, what seemed to us to be his power over life and death. And when he snapped open that little black bag, revealing row upon row of multicolored pills, I knew that he had to do some rearranging when he brought the babies. But I knew that the doctor could do it, because doctors could do anything.

I have not been alone in my wrong thinking about the source of life. Many people, even reputable scientists of old, at one time thought that maggots emerged directly from decayed meat, and that mice came automatically from old rags. It was known as the theory of spontaneous generation. Later, of course, we accepted the fact that life begets life.

And so where do insects come from? Today

most children are not as ignorant about the origin of insects as I was about how baby brother arrived on the scene. If one is observant, it is not too difficult to find insects in the process of mating. For several years we raised the silkworm moth, feeding the larvae on mulberry leaves from the backyard. After they had grown, spun their cocoon, and emerged as adults, the fertilization of the female by the male was the next scheduled act. Eggs laid by a nonfertilized female were not expected to hatch into larvae. We say they are sterile. Our children noted the fertilization process which involved the male and female. They skipped the doctor's little black bag theory for the generation of life.

They noted a similar process in the raising of chickens. If a flock of chickens was composed of all hens, we expected to have eggs for eating purposes, but not for "setting" purposes. A rooster was necessary to fertilize the female's eggs so that they would hatch into baby chicks.

However, there is a process known as parthenogenesis, a process of which I first learned in a study of insects. It is the word I shared with my friend who could not accept the virgin birth of Jesus Christ.

Although I have found squash bugs and butterflies "glued" together, the male in the process of injecting sperm into the female so that her eggs will be fertile, I learned that some insects do not go through this seemingly demanding process.

The best example of the exception to nature's normal action in this regard is found among the honey bees. When the queen lays an egg, if it is fertilized by one of the stored sperm that she received in her nuptial flight, it develops into a worker bee. If it is *not* fertilized, it develops into a drone bee. Without any question, the drone develops minus the help of the male. In that sense it is of virgin birth.

A number of other insects are also able to produce offspring without the aid of the male. Aphids must do this periodically because for a time only females are born. If the aphids are to continue during that time when the female completely dominates the life cycle, the young must be born without fertilization. And the female aphid goes it alone. Instead of laying eggs, she switches to production of her young alive. And it is done without the aid of any sperm. There are no males around.

Parthenogenesis is not just found among insects where it is the exclusive method of reproduction in some parasitic wasps and thrips. It is an occasional method of reproduction in some members of all major groups of animals except vertebrate (backboned) and echinoderms (starfish and the like).

So parthenogenesis, the production of young without male fertilization is very much with us. Parthenocarpy, the production of fruit without pollination, was chemically induced in cucumbers in the early 1970s. Parthenocarpy leads to the development of seedless fruit.

In the science laboratory the ova of frogs and even of rabbits have been stimulated to develop without fertilization. It has even occurred naturally in a new breed of turkeys, although development rarely continues to maturity.

I talked to my friend later. She had looked up the word, parthenogenesis, but was reluctant to discuss the implications of it with her doubt about the virgin birth of Jesus Christ.

I look at it like this. If parthenogenesis, the giving birth of young without fertilization, can occur normally in some insect species and other more highly developed animals, if it can occur in more advanced life with man's help, why could it not occur in Mary at God's direction?

My God is more advanced than any scientist. My God is not limited by nature. My God could send Jesus into this world in a parthenogenic way.

Sometimes people feel and express sorrow at my gullibility. And I in turn feel sorry for them because of their lack of faith.

Now the birth of Jesus Christ took place in this way. When his mother Mary had been betrothed to Joseph, before they came together she was found to be with child of the Holy Spirit. Matthew 1:18.

29

The Scuba Divers

If you take a large grasshopper and examine his long flexible abdomen, you will find on each side a series of pores (small openings), one per body segment. They are called spiracles and are the external openings of the insect's respiratory system. The openings connect with trachea, which are small air tubes. These branch and re-branch to all parts of the insect's body. Since we take in oxygen through our nasal passages, it seems rather strange that insects breath through their stomach area! I imagine, however, that if insects understand how we humans respire, they would find our breathing apparatus equally odd.

The respiratory system of the insect may seem simple and abnormal, but it is an efficient one. It is one of the reasons why insects are relatively stronger than man. Tests have shown that every time a grasshopper "takes a breath" there is a 20 percent renewal of oxygen in the hind leg! That's far better than happens in man.

But how do the insects make it who live in the water—insects like the giant waterbug, the back swimmer, the water boatman? The water strider is not involved here since he "skates" around on the surface of the water, but the three we mentioned plus others like them go on dives below that surface that may run up to 36 hours in length. How can they make it?

Very simply, yet very ingeniously. Most aquatic adult insects carry a supply of fresh air with them, trapping an air bubble under their wing covers or in some cases the air is simply trapped beneath tiny water-repellent hairs on the surface of their body. So they carry their own scuba tanks with them.

But they go man one better in this respect. Insects can replenish their own scuba tanks! The air they trap is like most air, basically 20 percent oxygen and 80 percent nitrogen. The oxygen is used by the insect and a bubble of nitrogen gas is left from the original air trapped. But there air is dissolved in the water. By a process which every biology student knows, osmosis, oxygen moves from the air dissolved in the water into the nitrogen bubble remaining. And thus the oxygen used by the insect is continually being replaced from the air dissolved in the water. Eventually the nitrogen in the insect's bubble of air is lost into the water and the insect must surface for a fresh supply of air. But still it is a remarkable feat, this extraction of oxygen from the water by the air-breathing insect.

I know of no Christian who survives by

himself, who is not dependent upon others, who needs not surface to have his basic spiritual needs replenished. There may be some such Christians, but I do not know of them personally. I am certain that they are few and far between, and probably pretty scrawny Christians at that.

As Christians we need to keep coming up for air. Perhaps as the water is to the insect we mentioned above, so the world is to us. We can be in that world, and God intended that we should be in it, but spiritual nourishment is limited in that world. If we do not upon occasion arise, draw ourselves apart to rest for a time like Jesus did, have our "oxygen" supply repleted, then we are in big trouble. In fact, I believe it is fatal. We mentioned how the water tends to absorb away the nitrogen part of the air bubble that the water boatman and the others carry with them. Eventually there is nothing left—no reserve, nothing for the oxygen from the water to dissolve into—and we drown in the world about us.

Christians surface from that world in the church. Here is a refuge, a gathering place for the saints. Here are Sunday school classes, sermons, messages in song that are like tonics to our bodies that have been tired by a week in the world. Some of us cannot make it for a week. We need midweek meetings. We must draw our spiritual refreshment from sources beyond the church.

But surely the church should be a main source of fresh "oxygen" for many. Some Christians say that they go to church to have their spiritual batteries recharged. The analogy is not bad. A battery changes chemical energy into electrical energy, but one dare not simply drain energy from it indefinitely. A battery needs to be recharged, regenerated, or it goes dead.

The story is told about a Christian who stopped coming to church. He thought he could make it just as well at home, listening to an occasional sermon on the radio, skipping the live contact and fellowship with other Christians.

His pastor came to visit him and they sat before the open fireplace, studying the flames, neither saying a word. Then the visiting pastor took a poker and drew a hot, glowing coal from the central mass of the fire. He pulled it apart from the rest until it stood alone upon the hearth, no glowing coals around it.

As they watched, the isolated, glowing coal slowly darkened and grew cold. The coals from which it had been withdrawn still glowed a cherry red.

The pastor, still saying nothing, rose to go. The wayward member who had gotten the point, shook the minister's hand and said, "I'll be back in church next Sunday."

We said that some of the water bugs ("bugs" is really a very sloppy name!) can make it for 36 hours in the water without surfacing. During that time they continue with all their normal bug functions and they gain a limited amount of oxygen from that dissolved in the water. Alert Christians can be supplied with some spiritual needs while in the world. After all, God is everywhere. But eventually they need that supply of oxygen refilled in more abundant fashion.

I do not know how long a Christian can exist as a Christian without contact, isolated from the believers. Some of God's choice servants have maintained their faith after long years of imprisonment. I believe there are exceptions to what we have been saying. Most of us, however, greatly need the fellowship, encouragement, and warmth of other Christians. I realize that the church is imperfect, that it is not just a sanctuary of the saints, but also a hospital for the sinners. Yet it is still the best source we have for finding that fellowship, encouragement, and warmth which we Christians must have.

Let us hold fast the confession of our hope without wavering for he who promised is faithful and let us consider how to stir up one another to love and good works, not neglecting to meet together, as is the habit of some, but encouraging one another, and all the more as you see the Day drawing near. Hebrews 10:23-25.

Slick
Suckers

In my teaching position I work with plants, often propagating them. Sometimes a young plant takes off beautifully, progresses, and I pat myself on the back with my green thumb.

But I have had plants suddenly lose interest in growth. Old leaves wilt, new growth stops, and it is obvious that we have a sick plant on our hands.

When we check out possible causes for the decline of the once healthy protégé, we find out that it is not due to our failure to provide water, light, and other necessities of life. Seemingly we have done our part, but the plant is failing to cooperate.

If we check the young plant carefully, we sometimes find cotton-like clusters on the plant, especially at the angles where the tiny branches meet the stem. And on lower leaves we may notice a glistening substance that is not being secreted by the leaf. Further examination reveals minute, soft-bodied creatures wandering around the ailing plant, often clinging to the underside of the leaves like criminals prowling dark alleys. We have found the vandals of our plant.

Our growth-stopper is the aphid or plant louse. These small insects have sucking mouth parts. They take plant juices directly from the plant in large volumes since the nutritive value of the sap for aphid subsistence is rather low. Excess fluids they excrete and this accounts for the glistening appearance on the upper surface of some of the leaves.

If we humans had cuts on our bodies from which blood dripped continuously, we would be like a plant suffering from an aphid infestation. The plant is being drained of vital liquids. No wonder it becomes weak, withers, and dies.

Aphids outdoors are often controlled by their natural enemies such as certain parasitic wasps, ladybird beetles, and various kinds of birds like warblers, chickadees, and vireos. But when aphids invade plants inside a home or green-house, then this advantage is lost.

Because of the "ants and their cows" relationship, aphids are sometimes considered to be cute and fascinating. Ants actually transport aphids to select portions of plants where they may feed, and then through stroking of the aphid's body encourage the secretive flow of "honey dew" from these tiny "cows." The secretion is then imbibed by the ants. This honey dew secretion is the cause of the leaf spotting we mentioned earlier. In the process of admiring the relationship, the cleverness of the ants, the symbiotic connection between the two whereby each receives benefits from the other, we sometimes overlook the harm they do to the plant.

Frankly, I have no admiration for the dairy cows of the ants. By sprays and hand washings (depending upon their numbers), I seek to eliminate them from my school greenhouse. And since they reproduce quickly, different generations of them having wings to facilitate their migration, one must be eternally on the alert.

When a young Christian stops growing, we need to check for the basics first. Is he receiving spiritual food? Is he continuing to drink of the water of life which Jesus advertised so clearly to the Samaritan woman in John 4 of the Bible? Is he devouring God's Word? Is he fellowshiping with other believers?

If the basics are all there, then we need to start looking for the unnoticed sin that is sucking away at his life. Satan is clever. Like the ants, he transports His sin aphids around, placing them upon tender tissue where they can grow and deprive the Christian of essentials that he needs for a balanced spiritual life. Like ants milking the aphids, so Satan profits when the Christian allows sin to fasten upon his life. First his spiritual growth begins to slow, then it plateaus, and finally it declines. Sin is never cute, and the Christian receives no benefits when he allows the evil one to pasture his sin cows upon him.

It is the duty of the Christian church to be observant of its members. Some plateaus in the Christian life may be normal, but let them serve as a clue, as a warning. If such a leveling off occurs in our life, or in the life of another in the fellowship, we should be willing to look more closely to see if a sin aphid is at work.

And as to the treatment? At school I have washed aphids off, sprayed them, or lightly touched them with an alcohol moistened swab. But in each case, action must be taken. Aphids are not wished away.

The blood of Jesus Christ can and does cleanse us from sin of the past, present, and future. But it must be claimed, for that forgiveness comes through acknowledgment and confession. Sometimes we need to take drastic action. No light touch with the alcohol swab will do it, but we must come publicly before our supporting fellowship. Like Alcoholics Anonymous, like Weight Watchers, the Christian fellowship becomes our examining, sustaining body.

Because of a high birthrate, because of population explosions, aphids have a way of quickly coming back into my once purged greenhouse. I must forever guard against them for they can suck my plants dry. Every Christian must be willing to examine himself, to subject himself to the discernment of the body of believers, to give counsel as well as receive counsel. By such actions we will cast off the sin that so easily besets us. We shall grow in our Christian life.

> Search me, O God, and know my heart!
> Try me and know my thoughts!
> And see if there be any wicked way in me
> and lead me in the way everlasting!
> Psalm 139:23, 24.

An
Insect
Thermometer

A project I like to have pupils attempt in biology is to find the "chirruper" of the cricket.

If students attempt this, they will need a male cricket, since the females are silent. Many caustic comments and sarcastic analogies could spring out of this choice tidbit of information, but a male chauvinist needs to be discrete amidst the women's liberation movement of the day. As far as I know, female crickets have made no protest because of their missing "vocal cords." Nor have the male crickets protested.

The female cricket is easily identified by the long needle like ovipositer which protrudes from her abdomen, lying between two hairlike projections of shorter length. The male, of course, lacks that middle projection.

If the fore (upper) wing is removed from the male and placed under a microscope, the student by searching near the front of that wing on the underside should find first what I often describe as a "broomstick with several dozen doughnuts threaded upon it." The heavy rib of the wing that we are describing is nicely enlarged by a 100-power microscope. The rib can be seen by the naked eye but it will take magnification to see the neat symmetry of the doughnut-like rings upon it. Each wing also has a scraper, a hard, sharp-edged portion that is of half circle shape. When the male cricket "sings," the front wings are raised so they are like a pitched roof over his body. He rubs his file (broomstick with doughnuts) with his scraper. This action sets his wings vibrating in rapid motion and his song fills the night air. That song has been described as *cree-cree, cree-cree; chee-chee, chee-chee;* or *re-treat, re-treat*. I like the first translation best since the call of the male is really his way of making advances toward the female. Certainly it is not a retreat.

Several years ago a male cricket found himself between the floor joists of our home. Each night he caroled madly for his true love who never appeared. Since the basement ceiling was not sealed off, it was possible to stand quietly on a chair and view his performance, wings vibrating too rapidly to be seen. I continued my observation for several nights, one male paying his respects to the vocalization of another, until my wife insisted the concert must stop.

As young fishermen we cared little about the chirrup of crickets. We were interested in them solely because we knew that a cricket on a hook at the end of a line attached to a bamboo pole was almost a sure bet to coax the "red eyes" (rock bass) in the St. Joseph River to bite. As a result we pulled in more than one fish regardless of the sex of the cricket.

Chirruping crickets often get up a chorus and quite nicely fall into what seems to be a natural rhythm, each participating cricket hitting the one-part harmony.

Another interesting fact about that chirrup is it varies with the temperature. In fact, it is said that if you count the cricket's chirrup for 13 seconds and add 40 you'll have the temperature in Fahrenheit degrees. Unfortunately, the snowy tree cricket is the most reliable of the cricket family to be used as a thermometer. For him the formula works very well. For the common black field cricket, the most common one around, the results are not so satisfactory. He is a better indicator on a fishhook for the presence of the "red eye" than he is for the temperature in the shrubbery outside the house.

There is no question, however, that the tempo of the insect's song steps up with the rise in temperature. As the weather cools off, the song decreases. There is a direct relationship between the temperature and the tempo. At first it sounds a bit insulting to the listening female. The ardor of her courter is more dependent upon the warmth of the air than the warmth he feels toward her. Actually, she is probably little bothered by his fickleness. As he serenades, she sometimes gives no more than a twitch of her antennae in his direction. There is no question that she hears since she has two good ears, one located on each *leg*! Probably she is playing hard to get.

Christians, both male and female, should be doing some chirruping. And most of us are. One wonders about the effect of temperature upon the tempo of our chirruping? And one might look at this "wonderment" from two different angles.

Perhaps one thing that governs the amount of the witness and praise coming from us who know the Lord is the warmth of our Christian experience.

If we are cold Christians, if nothing is happening in our lives, perhaps we have little to say to the world about us. Our output is low. And I can see why. We usually talk about the things we are enthusiastic about. The warmer the Christian experience, the more frequent the witness. Again we find that direct relationship.

The other aspect of this temperature business as it relates to the Christian witness causes us to look outside our own personal Christian experience and consider our reaction to external pressures.

Upon occasion the heat is put on a Christian from the world, not from the Spirit working within us. This heat is sometimes known as persecution. And when it occurs, what is our reaction? Do we speed up our trilling, or do we grow more silent?

As Christians, anxious not to offend others, perhaps we are too easily rebuffed by a bit of flack from the sinner. We have an innate tendency to clam up rather than open up. Our

168

Christian modesty and humility may dominate us at times to too great an extent.

Martyrs Mirror, a book we referred to earlier that deals with persecution of the Anabaptists of Europe in the 1500s, is not illustrative of "clamming up." Those earlier Christians had a way of going to their death so joyfully, with praises and testimony ringing from their lips, that their persecuters sometimes had their tongues removed to prevent joyful expressions escaping as the flames leaped about them and snuffed out their lives.

We have suggested that the male cricket chirrups to attract a mate, his chirrup regulated by the temperatures of his surroundings. If he is warm, he chirrups more rapidly. If cold, he slows down.

Every Christian should consider the reason for his witness, for its frequency. Are we "chirruping" to win people to Christ? Doesn't the warmth of one's Christian experience have a bearing upon that witness? If the pressure is on us, if persecution comes, does it mean that our Christian chirrup drops to zero?

When Jesus asked us to witness for Him, He made no allowance for temperature changes. He simply said, "You shall receive power when the Holy Spirit has come upon you; and you shall be my witnesses." Failure to appropriate the Holy Spirit may be the cause of our low chirruping rates, even our silence.

An exciting development has occurred recently. Charismatic people, those more richly blessed by the Holy Spirit, have seemingly become less reticent in regard to their "chirrup-ing." We are hearing more in the way of "Praise the Lord" serenading. Perhaps our increase in this respect will result in more sinners falling in love with the Christ we sing about. Always, however, we need to be certain that our "chirrup-ing" is for His honor and glory. We desire not that sinners fall in love with us, but rather with that lovely One from Galilee.

I will extol thee, my God and King,
    and bless thy name for ever and ever.
Every day I will bless thee,
    and praise thy name for ever and ever.

Psalm 145:1, 2.

APPENDIX

Insect Orders

A listing of ten major and ten minor insect orders, with a brief description of each order and with examples.

MAJOR ORDERS

1. Coleoptera

    Two pair of wings, upper pair being hard and shell-like. Complete metamorphosis (having four life stages: egg, larva, pupa, and adult). All beetles belong to this order. Both adult and larva have chewing mouthparts. *Examples*: June beetle, ladybird beetle, firefly.

2. Diptera

    One pair of wings, one pair of "balancing organs" known as *halteres* and located just behind wings. Complete metamorphosis. Contains the flies, most members possessing piercing-sucking mouthparts. *Examples*: housefly, mosquito, crane fly.

3. Hemiptera

    The true "bugs" belong in this order, usually having four wings, the front pair being thick at the base, thin at the tips, and overlapping each other as they are folded flat on the back. They have piercing-sucking mouthparts, incomplete metamorphosis (life stages of egg, nymph, and adult). *Examples*: stinkbug, water strider, bedbug.

4. Homoptera

   An order with members that vary widely in appearance. If wings are present, they are held rooflike over the body, front wings may be transparent. They have piercing-sucking mouthparts and incomplete metamorphosis. *Examples*: treehopper, cicada, aphid, mealybug.

5. Hymenoptera

   Bees and wasps belong to this order. Four wings, chewing mouthparts with lower lip often developed into a "tongue." Frequenters of flowers with complete metamorphosis, "social" insects. *Examples:* Honeybee, ant, bumblebee, mud-dauber wasp.

6. Isoptera

   Contains the termites or "white ants." They are distinguished from the ants by not having the pinched-in waist. They have incomplete metamorphosis, chewing mouthparts, feeding on wood, *Example*: termite

7. Lepidoptera

   Characterized by the moths and butterflies, siphoning mouthparts, two pair of wings, complete metamorphosis. *Examples:* monarch butterfly, cecropia moth, silverspotted skipper.

8. Odonata

   Large insects having four long, many-veined wings of about equal size, chewing mouthparts. Incomplete metamorphosis. *Examples*: dragonfly, damselfly.

9. Orthoptera

> Usually with four wings, the front pair being narrow and leatherly, the hind pair are large and fold up like a fan under the front wings. Chewing mouthparts and incomplete metamorphosis. *Examples*: grasshopper, cricket, cockroach, praying mantis.

10. Siphonaptera

> Small, wingless insects with piercing-sucking mouthparts, complete metamorphosis, parasitic. *Example*: flea.

MINOR ORDERS

1. Anoplura

> Wingless, flat-bodied insects, sucking mouthparts, develop without metamorphosis, the life stages being egg, young, and adult. Parasitic. *Example*: louse.

2. Collembola

> Small, wingless, leaping insects. Without metamorphosis, chewing mouthparts, and with the ability to flip themselves into the air by means of a spring-like organ on the underside of the abdomen. *Example:* springtails.

3. Dermaptera

> Small insects, usually with four wings, the front pair short, leaving most of the abdomen exposed. Chewing mouthparts and incomplete metamorphosis. Very seclusive. *Example*: earwigs.

4. Ephemerida

> An order containing the mayflies, short lived

as adults. Incomplete metamorphosis. Two pair of triangular, many-veined wings. Two or three long antennae-like appendages at the end of the abdomen. *Example*: mayflies.

5. Mallophaga

   Wingless, flat-bodied insects, parasitic on birds and to some extent on mammals. Chewing mouthparts, feeding on hair, feathers, scales, and dried blood. Life stages of egg, young, and adult. *Example:* chicken louse.

6. Neuroptera

   Medium to large size insects with four many-veined wings. Chewing mouthparts, frequently with long antennae. Complete metamorphosis, all four life stages of egg, larva, pupa, and adult. *Examples*: dobsonfly, green lacewings, and ant lion.

7. Plecoptera

   Four pairs of wings with hind pair much larger than front pair, incomplete metamorphosis. Chewing mouthparts but many of the adults do not feed, long antennae. *Example*: stone flies.

8. Thysanoptera

   Tiny insects with or without wings. Rasping-sucking mouthparts, feeders on plants. Incomplete metamorphosis. *Example*: thrips.

9. Thysanura

   The bristletails are fast running, wingless, fish-shaped insects. They have long antennae and two or three long antennae-like appendages at the end of their abdomen.

Without metamorphosis, chewing mouth-parts, sometimes household pests. *Examples*: silverfish and firebrat.

10. Trichoptera
    Four-winged, mothlike insects having long slender antennae. Complete metamorphosis, chewing mouthparts. *Example*: caddis fly.

A majority of the characteristics listed above for each order of insects was taken from the pamphlet, *Insects—How to Collect, Preserve and Identify Them*. This helpful publication is Extension Bulletin 352 from the Agricultural Extension Service of Purdue University, Lafayette, Indiana. The authors are G. E. Lehker and H. O. Deay.

SELECTED BIBLIOGRAPHY

Amos, William H. *The Life of the Pond*. New York:Mcgraw-Hill Book Co., 1967.

Barker, Will. *Familiar Insects of America*. New York: Harper and Brothers Publishers, 1960.

Calahan, Philip. *Insects and How They Function*. New York: Holiday House, 1971.

_____ *Insect Behavior.*New York: Four Winds Press, 1970.

Curran, Dr.C. H. *Insects in Your Life*. New York: Sheridan House, 1951.

Dupuy, William Atherton. *Our Insect Friends and Foes*. New York: Dover Publications, 1940.

Farb, Peter, and the editors of Life-Time, Inc. *The Insects*. New York, 1962.

Gaul, Albro T. *The Wonderful World of Insects*. New York: Rinehart and Co., Inc., 1953.

Grosvenor, Gilbert. *Our Insect Friends and Foes and Spiders*. Washington D.C.: National Geographic Society, 1935.

Harpster, Hilda. *Insect World*. New York: Viking Press, 1948.

Hopf, Alice L. *Monarch Butterflies*. New York: Thomas Y. Crowell Co., 1965.

Hutchins, Rose E. *Insects*. Englewood Cliffs, N.J.: Prentice-Hall, Inc., 1966.

_____ *The Ant Realm*. New York: Dodd, Mead & Co., 1967.

Hylander, Clarence J. *Insects on Parade*. New York: Macmillan Co., 1957.

Kalmus, H. *101 Simple Experiments with Insects*. Garden City, N.Y.: Doubleday and Co., Inc., 1960.

Klots, Alexander B. and Elsie B. Klots. *Living Insects of the World*. Garden City, N.Y.: Doubleday and Co., Inc., 1959.

_____ *1001 Questions Answered About Insects*. New York: Dodd, Mead and Co., Inc., 1961.

Lanham, Url. *The Insects*. New York: Columbia University Press, 1964.

Larson, Peggy Pickering and Mervin W. Larson. *Lives of Social Insects*. New York: The World Publishing Co., 1968.

Lutz, Frank E. *A Lot of Insects*. New York: G. P. Putman's Sons, 1941.

Neider, Charles. *The Fabulous Insects*. New York: Harper and Brothers, Publishers, 1954.

Newman, L. H. *Man and Insects*. Garden City, N.Y.: Natural History Press, 1966.

Pringle, Lawrence, *Pests and People*. New York: Macmillan Co., 1972.

Rhine, Richard. *Life in a Bucket of Soil*. New York: Lothrop, Lee and Shepard Co., 1972.

Shackelford, Frederick. *Insect Stories*. San Francisco: Harr Wagner Publishing Co., 1940.

Shuttlesworth, Dorothy. *Natural Partnerships*. Garden City, N.Y.: Doubleday and Co., 1969.

Simon, Hilda. *Our Six-Legged Friends and Allies*. New York: Vanguard Press, Inc., 1971.

Smith, Howard G. *Tracking the Unearthly Creatures of Marsh and Pond*. Nashville, Tenn.: Abington Press, 1972.

Teale, Edwin Way. *Grassroots Jungles*. New York: Dodd, Mead & Co., 1937.

_____ *The Strange Life of Familiar Insects*. New York: Dodd, Mead & Co., 1962.

Urquart, F. A. *Introducing the Insect*. New York: Henry Holt & Co., 1949.

Wigglesworth, V. B. *The Life of Insects*. New York: The World Publishing Co., 1964.

past thirty-five years, frequently under a pseudonym.

He is the author of *God Healed Me*, which tells the stories of twenty-four persons who have sought divine healing. An earlier book of short stories, *Second Chance*, is no longer in print. He has served as associate editor of the *Gospel Evangel* for more than a decade and his weekly column for Sunday school teachers has appeared in *Builder* since January 1965.

Married and the father of five, Baker has taught on the junior high level for the Elkhart Community Schools for twenty-eight years. He worships at the Belmont Mennonite Church of Elkhart where he has been an active layman for the past forty-four years.

ROBERT J. BAKER, a native of the Hoosier state, was
born in Goshen, Indiana, and has lived for many years
in nearby Elkhart. He received the BA degree from
Goshen College, Goshen, Indiana; the MS degree from
Indiana University, Bloomington, Indiana; and the
MAT degree from Michigan State University, East
Lansing, Michigan. He completed further graduate
training at Emory University, Atlanta, Georgia, Ball
State University, Muncie, Indiana and the Indiana
State University, Terre Haute, Indiana.

Baker's first written material was published in 1937
in a school anthology for students at Elkhart High
School. Hundreds of his short stories, articles, and
poems have appeared in the religious press during the